A GOOD MAN

A GOOD MAN

ANI KATZ

THORNDIKE PRESS
A part of Gale, a Cengage Company

Copyright © 2020 by Ani Katz.
Thorndike Press, a part of Gale, a Cengage Company.

Thorndike Press® Large Print Bill's Bookshelf.
The text of this Large Print edition is unabridged.
Other aspects of the book may vary from the original edition.
Set in 16 pt. Plantin.

LIBRARY OF CONGRESS CIP DATA ON FILE.
CATALOGUING IN PUBLICATION FOR THIS BOOK
IS AVAILABLE FROM THE LIBRARY OF CONGRESS

ISBN-13: 978-1-4328-7793-4 (hardcover alk. paper)

Published in 2020 by arrangement with Penguin Books, an imprint of Penguin Publishing Group, a division of Penguin Random House, LLC

Printed in Mexico
Print Number: 01   Print Year: 2020

For my grandparents:
Murray, a mensch
and Lillian, a lover of opera

The billy club arrived with the first shipment of Christmas presents that year, one package among several stacked on the front porch. The snow had started in the late afternoon, and by the time I got home from work the lawn was dusted with powder. The girls were still out — ballet maybe, or a violin lesson. In the hush of the early dark, I knelt and gathered the gifts in my arms, then carried them into our house.

The club had made the long journey coastward from the home of an amateur craftsman in War Eagle, Arkansas, who'd advertised the club on eBay as an absolutely terrific tire and fish thumper. Carved from Ozark red cedar, the club was about the size of a T-ball bat, and it had a nice old-fashioned look to it, like something you'd hang in your study instead of your garage. Wrapped around the rich wood barrel, held in place by a rubber band, there was a sheet

7

of paper — a letter from the seller, which I lost almost immediately. The missive must have been shuffled in with the old school flyers and grocery lists and holiday cards, tossed out with the rest of the paper ephemera that was always blanketing the kitchen counter.

But I remember most of what the letter said. It was a testimony of faith, one man's deliverance from death through the power of prayer. Stricken by pancreatic cancer, the seller had given up on life, but one day his wife had dragged him to church — long-sleeved in the August heat, trying to hide the yellowing of his skin — and there in the pew he had a revelation. He saw his entire life pass before his eyes, and that's when he knew that he was being protected by a power greater than himself. He began to weep. And when he got into his car to go home, he looked down and the yellow in his skin had disappeared. A few days later, his doctor told him his tumor was gone.

The seller signed off by calling me brother. He said my name was a blessing, that Thomas the apostle had doubted the Resurrection, but found his faith when he touched Christ's wounded body — a miracle! (I have seen the Caravaggio painting of the subject: old doubting Thomas, his forehead creased with awe as Christ grasps his wrist and guides his hand to his bloodless breast, one calloused finger probing the dark gap where the spear went in.) The prophet from War Eagle said that I should not doubt, that mercy was real, and my own miracle would come soon.

I remember reading the letter at the kitchen island, my dog nosing at my ankles, asking for his dinner. I had switched on Met Opera Radio — as I always did the moment I got home — and while I bore witness to this stranger's supposed healing and salvation and his promise of my own, I was treated to the end of the first act of *Eugene Onegin*. (It was the splendid 1992 Bychkov recording; Hvorostovsky is impeccable in the title role.) I folded the letter away as my wife and daughter bustled in through the side door, the sweet jangle of their chatter and the dog's exuberant yelps drowning out Onegin's warnings to Tatyana about self-control and inexperience, my dear girls' voices mingling with the chorus of the maids singing blithely in the garden, cold air exhaling off their bodies as they greeted me, the dog hurling himself at our shins.

Swimming. It had been swimming. I remember my daughter's wet hair, her dark curls still stringy and sodden against her neck and collar — the chlorine on her skin when she kissed me.

Earlier that year my agency had done a television spot for a cancer drug that supposedly added six months or more to the life spans of truly hopeless cases. The ad opens with a scene of a Mr. Rogers type, struggling to rouse himself from an easy chair, looking fretfully at the stoic face of the clock on the wall. Then it cuts to a woman escorting her elderly mother down a hall, their faces grim. That scene gives way to a handsome man lying in bed, too tired to notice his wife tidying around him.

These are the sick, the nearly dead, their worlds cool and colorless.

But then a sunburst comes sparkling into view, a constellation of gold that forms the name of the miracle drug. Honeyed droplets scatter and suffuse the air of each tableau, bringing life to each lost cause.

Now the Mr. Rogers type is sitting at a newly renovated kitchen counter, playing a game on a digital tablet with his grandson. His own son is chopping vegetables, sneaking a fond gaze at his old man. Now the woman is walking with her mother on a quaint downtown street lined with cherry blossom trees, their faces masks of bliss.

Now the handsome man is waltzing with his wife at an outdoor wedding, his hand pressed to the small of her back. They are all alive, defiantly so.

In the last shot, these people find themselves gathered in a summer field, drawn together by some powerful, benevolent force. They look around, smiling cautiously, unsure if they know each other, but certain they belong there. Before them is a glowing golden obelisk, carved with the miracle drug's name. They all reach out their hands and step into the light.

That's what I did for a living. I spun stories, made things like death seem clean and manageable — attractive, even.

I don't really believe in any of it, of course. God, miracles, any of those fantasies. I believe in medicine and advertising, but even those realities aren't infallible. Sometimes the drug doesn't work. Sometimes people see through the story you're trying to sell.

The most earnest expression of faith I can tolerate is Wagner's masterpiece *Tannhäuser*. The titular hero of the opera is a talented court singer in thirteenth-century Germany, and when we first meet him he is ensconced in the sensual grotto of Venus, the pagan goddess of love and lust. Tannhäuser's appetites have finally been satisfied, and he longs for the wholesome joys of the world he left behind: the soft air of spring and the sound of church bells. He returns to the world of mortals, waking up in a valley outside the city and looking on in gratitude as a chorus of pilgrims passes by on their way to Rome. Tannhäuser's fellow singers welcome him back into court; the noble-hearted Wolfram persuades him by telling him that the virginal Elisabeth has been pining over him ever since he left. She will be overjoyed to see him again.

It should be a happy homecoming, but our histrionic hero cannot help himself. Invited to participate in a singing contest about the nature of love, he breaks into a hymn of wanton ecstasy, exposing his sins to all assembled. The court is appalled, and they condemn Tannhäuser to death, but saintly Elisabeth shields him with her body, crying out that the wretch must be allowed to seek salvation through atonement. He must make his own pilgrimage to Rome, and only then will he have the chance to be absolved.

As the curtain rises on the final act, it is evening in the valley. Autumn. Months have passed, and the good Wolfram watches poor Elisabeth pray, clinging to her last hopes.

They hear the pilgrims approach, returning from Rome. As they sing of their journey Elisabeth searches each face, looking for Tannhäuser, but he is not among the faithful. She kneels in defeat; though Wolfram tries to guide her home, she tells him that her path leads toward heaven. She must intercede directly with God to save the man she loves.

At last Tannhäuser appears, haggard and pale. He tells Wolfram he has failed, that when he reached Rome and sought absolution from the pope, he was forever damned with an awful decree: *As this staff in my hand, no more shall bear fresh leaves, from the hot fires of hell, salvation never shall bloom for thee.*

Tannhäuser cries out for Venus, but Wolfram saves him by speaking Elisabeth's name, breaking the spell once and for all. As dawn comes over the valley, the funeral procession approaches, bearing Elisabeth's body. Tannhäuser kneels over her, begging with his last breath for her to pray for him. Through the death of the woman who loved him most, he has been redeemed. As our hero dies and the final curtain begins to fall, a young boy runs onstage wielding a flowering staff for all to see.

End of opera.

It's a sublime story of redemption. Even so, I find myself wondering whether it is actually an indictment of belief, a heart-breaking display of its limits. After all, the staff blooms with new flowers only after our hero has died.

So no, I cannot really say that I am a believer. I suppose I believe in mercy, most of the time, although I doubt I deserve it.

Even though I'm not a believer, for some reason I regret losing that letter from the man in War Eagle. I've often felt that if I could have it back, if I could just see the specifics of its language and revisit its turns of phrase, it would give me some answers about that time in my life. The letter had a crude poetry to it, a certain innocent passion that touched me, somehow. Re-creating it here, I know I've missed the heart of it.

I've considered writing to the man and asking him to send me another copy, but for all I know he's now dead of his supposedly cured cancer. I don't want to find out.

And of course, the letter could be nothing like I remember. Like an incantation in a dream that proves meaningless in the morning. I don't want to find that out either.

The billy club was for protection. Psychological protection, at least. There was a lot to worry about in those days. There were

14

the things that horrified everyone, of course: assault rifle massacres at office parties, little girls blown to pieces at pop concerts. Everyone could agree that kind of operatic bloodshed was terrible.

But there were other things that inspired a different kind of fear, things that felt like lead coiled in my gut — the subtler signs of impending catastrophe. Like the paramilitary policemen — America's own *Schutzstaffel* — mixed in with the naked cowboys and Mickey Mice and painted ladies in Times Square, close to my office, or the gaunt hunger strikers camped out in the international terminals of airports. Even worse, there were the things that you didn't see out in the world, things that wouldn't even make it onto the news — the things you had to find out for yourself on message boards, down rabbit holes of hyperlinks, reading with parched eyes long after midnight. The dread of all that never went away, and it was easy to believe that my life as I knew it was just a paper facade, waiting to be punctured by horrors that could take me from my family — or worse, take my family from me.

My girls would have told you I wasn't paranoid or crazy. They might have joked about it, sure — my wife rolling her eyes, my daughter screwing her pretty face into that tasted-a-lemon look she'd paste on when she thought something was funny or ridiculous.

Daddy, she'd admonish me. Don't be so *silly.*

I could be silly, but I wasn't crazy. Our lives were good — great, even. We were happy and secure. We had everything we needed.

There was no way for anyone to know — least of all me — that it would all end the way it did.

You've seen us, I'm sure — in the newspapers, on television, on the web. You've probably seen the photograph of us on the beach, even though it's at least two or three years out of date. It's sunset, so the flash is on, bleaching out the angel wings of our white linen shirts and highlighting the rosy clouds over the slate ocean behind us. My wife is farthest from the camera, laughing as she begins to peel away from us toward the surf, her slender left arm thrown out in some kind of salute. My daughter is between us, her arms linked tightly with ours, grinning with missing teeth. She was nine or ten, I think. And I'm in the foreground, trying to look dignified, my chin raised in satisfaction and my eyes bright with pride.

That's me. That's us. It feels like another life now.

Everyone uses the same photo, and they all write increasingly far-fetched variations on the same themes. It seems that after the initial flurry of coverage — after the piece-by-piece assembly of the picture puzzle of events — each new analysis must justify its existence with the promise of fresh insight. They use words like *self-righteous, paranoid, disappointed, anomic.* They write of revenge, of altruism — of the plight of women and the plight of men. And so on and so on forever and ever, because the puzzle is always incomplete. The pieces refuse to fit; the mirror stays fogged.

I used to keep up with what was written, but after a while I got tired of all the competing mutations of the story. None of them were ever quite true.

I have my own struggles with understanding exactly what happened. Sometimes I think I am a victim of circumstance. Sometimes I think I am a monster. Most often, I think I am like Tannhäuser himself — a deeply flawed man who sacrifices everything in an act of desperation, a sinner who can only gain salvation through the death of his most beloved.

Of course, I know it's unforgivable to

17

speak of my own pain. How can I even admit that I suffer, when I can still see their faces before me?

Then again, I am the only one who can tell this story. I am the only one who can speak of the tragedy that befell us.

I know it would make more sense to start at the beginning. That's how these things always start. The problem is that I'm not sure where the story really begins — how far back I have to go to find the rotted root, deep down in the blackened soil. It may have begun with the billy club, or with the other terrible things that happened that year. Or it may have started even earlier than that. Maybe it began with the happy years with my wife and daughter, or even in my own childhood.

I've never liked beginning new projects. It has always felt like hiking up a hill under a low gray sky, standing around a featureless clearing. I can build anything, and nothing stands in my way, but I have no idea where, or how, to begin. Every choice feels hollow and insufficient, like kicking up clouds of silt that settle back into the ground.

I'm much happier, much more sure of myself, once the structure is built. It may have problems, but now I can fix them. I've built a house that I know how to enter. I know where the rooms are, and what I will find in them. If I close my eyes I can feel my way around, find what I've misplaced, add what needs adding. I'm safe within those walls, secure with what I've accomplished so far. I wander around, making improvements.

We did not live in the house that my great-grandfather had built. That crumbling Victorian still belonged to my mother and my spinster sisters, and they played at being some kind of family within its walls, captives to its grand decrepitude.

My girls and I lived half an hour away on the North Shore in a tidy white Dutch Colonial with three bedrooms, a new kitchen, a gravel driveway, and a manageable mortgage. When I met my wife I had just begun to save for a house like this, working long hours at the office in Midtown, but my wife's trust fund was what made it possible for us to have our dream home in the suburbs while we were still young enough to enjoy the feeling of our own lawn beneath our feet.

Before our daughter was born, my wife sometimes complained that we couldn't buy the nice kind of toilet paper, or have internet in our one-bedroom garden apartment a gentrified block away from the Gowanus Houses in Brooklyn.

That's what the library is for, I would tell her.

It was her money, she would complain. Why couldn't she spend it the way she wanted to?

And then I would have to remind her that ultimately we both wanted the same things, and we were supposed to be on the same team, and that would be the end of it.

Back then I was making high five figures, but my wife wasn't working. We tried to be fair about negotiating our spending and our saving, but it could be hard, especially because my wife wasn't used to doing without all the little luxuries she was accustomed to. I loved the cozy feeling of a growing balance. She wanted her toilet paper.

Eventually she just started paying for the internet herself. I don't even remember having a conversation about it. One day bills began to arrive, and they were in her name.

This all seems like an unnecessary tangent. But days return to me, unfurling in my memory like parts of a film: images and scenes, borrowed and spliced, more real than reality. Even when they don't seem to tell a story, even when I'm not sure what they mean, they feel significant, somehow.

We should begin where my life really began, that year of firsts — the first night I met Miriam, the first sweet and effervescent months of our life together, the first time I brought her home with me. Miriam, my Miri — the woman who would become my wife.

We may as well begin there.

I

She found me at the bar on my corner. The oldest bar in Brooklyn, according to her dog-eared guidebook. It wasn't exactly what she had expected. She adored the stained glass windows and all the old mahogany — like the choir of a cathedral, she said — but she was disappointed they didn't serve cocktails.

At least *you* came along, she laughed, once we were a few rounds in and had gotten friendly with each other. She touched my arm, letting her fingertips linger in the crook of my elbow, blushing at her own boldness.

I can still see myself there, seeing her for the first time. I had stopped in for a nightcap after an arduous day at the office, and at first I was convinced I had made a mistake. On Thursdays the bar was always a madhouse, and on that night it was so crowded, so chaotic, that I almost turned around and walked out.

Then I saw her. She was perched by herself at the bend of the broad wooden bar, her dark head bent over her book as bodies blundered around her, careless voices flaring like firelight against the walls. She alone was serene, unbothered by the bedlam — the signal in the noise. I took the empty stool beside her, and she looked up at me, her face warmed with a garnet glow from the window above. She smiled.

My Miriam.

Since they didn't serve cocktails, we made do with whiskey. One, and another, and another. I paid for it all. We inched closer to each other on our barstools, our kneecaps locking together like a well-worn wooden toy.

She told me about her childhood in Paris. Her maternal grandparents owned a successful kosher butcher shop on the cobblestoned Rue des Rosiers in the increasingly posh Marais; as a child, she'd spent long afternoons and Sundays helping out around the store, learning the cycles of soaking and salting to draw the blood from the meat. When she thought of home, she didn't see her parents — a stern obstetrician and a depressed housewife prone to migraines — or their small, heirloom-filled apartment

24

near Place des Vosges, but rather her grand-father in a spotless white apron, her grand-mother handling money with a kerchief tied over her hair, ruby slabs of beef, thick knobs of lamb shanks, pale chicken parts nestled like newborn kittens.

Desperate to get away from home, she had gone to the University of Provence, several hours south of where she grew up. There she studied Courbet and the other realists, smoked cigarettes, slept with men, ate formerly forbidden foods like moules-frites and pork sausage. She worked as a waitress, a barback, a nanny, but only when she needed more cash than her monthly allow-ance could provide.

At twenty-five she gained access to her trust fund and could begin to travel — weekends in Barcelona and London, a month in Rome, always on her own. This was her first trip to the States, though she'd been to Montreal once before. She was in New York for a little more than a week, but she wished she could stay longer.

But why alone? I asked. Why not with friends? Aren't you lonely?

Why should I need anyone else? They would just hold me back.

I told her my own story — a version of it, anyway. I glossed over my childhood on

Long Island, flat land of strip malls and forever-flooded basements, leaving out all the meaningful details. I spoke of my scholarship to Amherst, my move to the city, my ascent from creative intern to junior art director.

I did not tell her that I had no plans to stay in Brooklyn, or that I only lived there because it was the accepted way station for young people who'd gone to good colleges. Brooklyn was just a stop before settling down.

And of course I did not tell her why I wanted to settle down so desperately, or why I ached to assume the status of husband and father. That would have required me to explain my own upbringing, and those hurts were far too ugly for a first encounter.

Later that night, I held her steady on the sidewalk as a bitter late-winter wind gusted through our open coats. I watched as she ate a chocolate bar I bought for her from the corner bodega and saw that her hand and lips were pale, that her eyes were unfocused but bright.

What do I owe you? she asked, the bodega's door jangling behind us as we stepped back into the night.

Owe me?

For the drinks and everything. You know.

She stumbled and caught herself, then leaned against me, her cheek snug on my shoulder.

Nothing, I laughed as I steered us toward my apartment. Don't be ridiculous.

At some point we had agreed that she should stay over — it wasn't safe for her to go back to her hotel alone, not at this hour. But it wasn't what you think. We got inside and immediately passed out on my bed, lights and clothes still on, without so much as a good night kiss. She was my guest, after all, a lone traveler looking for safety — a lady — and I was too much of a gentleman to expect anything else would happen that night.

It wasn't until the early morning that she unfurled her sleep-warmed body against mine, and then we made love for the first of many times that dreamlike week — the first week of our lives together. She was so tender, so elated in her yielding to me, and when it was over and we lay beside each other with my hand still gripped in hers, I couldn't believe what I had found.

That afternoon I called a car and we took a quick trip into the West Village to retrieve her bag from her hotel, and after that she hardly left my apartment for days. She would stay in bed when I went to work in the mornings, and I would keep that image in my mind, hungering for her. When I came home in the evenings she would still be lolling around in her underwear, sometimes reading my books, sometimes listening to one of the opera records I had played for her, sometimes cooking for us. I'd take her in my arms and the sauce would burn.

I've wanted you all day, I would say.

The truth was, I had known from the moment I saw her that it was all out of my control — that no matter what I did from then on, there was no question in my mind that she was going to come into my life and change it forever.

She was supposed to fly back to Paris the following Monday, but that Sunday night over the dinner I'd made for us she put down her fork and looked up at me with shining doe eyes.

I don't want to go home.

Then don't, I said. Stay here.

But I only have a tourist visa.

Just stay as long as you can, I said. We'll figure things out.

I knew I was being impulsive. But I also knew that I wanted to keep her.

You mean it?

Of course.

She moved in. I already had most everything we needed, but I let her add her own little touches to the place — a few succulents and a fiddle-leaf fig, some framed prints from the Met Store, a new leather club chair that we picked out together. And of course there were her dresses filling half of our closet and her soft lace underthings spilling out of the laundry hamper, the shared showers and meals and daily chores. Before long, it felt like a real home that we had built together with mutual care and intention, so very unlike the home where I had grown up, where my parents could neither make each other happy nor keep their children safe from their particular expressions of misery — a home where it had always been so difficult to breathe.

My life with Miriam couldn't have been further from that stifling morass, and our partnership was the polar opposite of my parents' unfortunate union. Other people envied us — we always looked like we were on top of the world when we were out together, and we made an undeniably attractive couple. At thirty, I was a slender six feet. My blond hair still flopped boyishly over my forehead, but I had a gray suit and a navy suit that fit me perfectly, and I carried myself like the man I was becoming. And Miriam was the *ideal woman.* I loved the way she knew how to wear red lipstick, her assurance on heels, the way her hips moved when she walked. I loved her quiet way of assessing a room, listening while absorbing everyone else's attention. I was always proud to be seen with her.

She met my college friends — the handful I'd kept in touch with — helped clear the table at dinner parties, chatted with the other girlfriends in galley kitchens (she got along so well with all the girls, even though she was the most sophisticated by far). She came to my company softball game in a yellow gingham sundress and a straw hat, a cold thermos of rosé in her tote bag. We went to the opera, went out dancing, went for brunch. In the dark, our heads on one pillow, I called her Miri.

I was in love. We were in love.

I know how hackneyed it must sound, but I had no idea that love could be like that. As children, my sister Evie and I had developed our notions of love from our father's opera recordings and our furtive readings of our mother's romance novels. We would play in Evie's bedroom, pretending to be Mimi and Rodolfo, Tristan and Isolde, or whichever generic man-woman combination we found clinched together in a paperback's pages.

That was our fiction of love. It took us a long time to understand why love — or what passed for it — looked so different in our own house: our father making French toast for family supper after a wrathful night and blacked-out morning, my mother staying with the twins in their bedroom long after they'd fallen asleep.

I told Miriam very little of this. We were moving inexorably toward a future together. The less said about the past, the better.

And then almost half a year had gone by, and we were traveling out to the overripe bayou of summertime Long Island not just to celebrate my mother's sixtieth birthday — the stated purpose of the visit — but so I could search the cluttered ruins of my childhood home for the diamond ring that had belonged to my father's grandmother and had graced the left hand of every married woman in my family since the early days of the century.

My mother had been the last to wear the ring, but not for over a decade now, and I had no idea what she'd done with it. I hoped that she was keeping it safe for me. More likely, it was buried somewhere in the bowels of her bedroom, where no one could find it.

Unless she had thrown it away.

When I remember that visit, I think of the drive out there — Miriam in the passenger seat, the streetlights grazing the tops of her bare knees as if they were rising up out of dark water. She'd been asleep since we'd turned onto Southern State. I'd planned to take the scenic route on the Ocean Parkway, so she could see the pockets of churning Atlantic peeking through the dunes, the red glow of the sunset spilled over the yawning calm of the bay, but since she had fallen asleep I decided to go the faster way.

We'd see the beach another time.

I glanced over and watched the streetlights slide over Miriam's body, the bright beams slicing across her bare throat. She had worn the short black chiffon wrap dress with the tiny white flowers, a good choice — it showed off her figure and didn't compete with the striking Picasso qualities of her face. On the radio, my favorite cast of *Le Nozze di Figaro:* Bryn Terfel merrily measuring out the space for his marital bed while Alison Hagley admires her bridal veil, her clarion soprano wreathed with joyous anticipation.

Without going into detail about the specific causes of dysfunction, I had warned

Miriam repeatedly what it would be like — the house, my family. To head off disaster, I had called my mother the week before and given her clear instructions for the weekend: what we as a family would talk about, and what we would absolutely not talk about.

Keep it light, I'd said, and my mother had pouted and huffed, claiming not to understand what I meant.

I exited the highway and we crested into town. Now I could hear the hush of the AC straining against the vents, the hum of the road beneath us. I kept the windows rolled up against the darkness of the town as we crossed from one side to the other — through the neighborhoods of small homes shadowed by the soaring highway overpass, over the dividing spine of the train tracks, past shuttered strip malls and lonely diners and the glowing prairies of car dealerships — until we reached downtown. The prosperous and leafy neighborhoods were near the water, south of Main Street, where the lampposts had wreaths at Christmastime. In a few more miles I made a right, headed down a long and winding lane where houses stayed hidden behind tall walls of shrubbery. Finally, the familiar rumble as we turned in to the gravel drive, passing under the low-hanging trees and to the house.

33

I watched Miriam stir and wake. She let out a little moan as she peered out into the darkness, then turned to me, eyes still squinted shut, stretching.

Well, sweetheart, I sighed. We're here.

Perhaps I should have warned her about everything once more. I probably should have apologized for bringing her into this house and foisting my family upon her, burdening her with her own role in our domestic drama. But I didn't, because I knew she would have told me not to worry.

The truth was we could handle anything as long as we were together.

I carried the bags in: our weekend duffel and the groceries from the specialty food store near our apartment, because I never arrived anywhere — not even my own childhood home — empty-handed. We clambered up the wide wooden porch and opened the double-hung Dutch door that was never locked, and suddenly we were standing in my front hall, confronted by our faces reflected in the greasy gilded mirror balanced on the foyer credenza, our passage into the house blocked by the heft of the wraparound staircase, which the members of the household were now bounding down.

Mommy, they're here!

My younger sisters, Deirdre and Katharine, though we always called them Deedee and Kit. The twins. They were painfully thin except for their cherubic faces; their light hair was wound into topknots, streaked with blue and ruby and amethyst. They were wearing pajamas — silky boxers and old T-shirts spattered with paint — but it was unclear if this was because they were going to bed or because that was what they'd worn all day.

They were twenty years old and considered themselves artists. Haphazardly home-schooled since the fourth grade, they were immature for their age — more like young teenagers than young adults. According to our mother, it made sense that they still lived at home. They were so *young,* she always said. Just little girls, really. How could anyone expect them to make their own way in the world when they'd been raised like veal calves, confined to a cage all their short lives?

The twins reached for Miriam, stroked her arms with quiet awe.

I've heard so much about you, Miriam said, and they drew back, suspicious.

Really?

Like what?

But before Miriam could explain, my mother was there, beaming at us with disagreeable intensity. She was a birdlike woman with yellowing teeth and ashen hair, the loose sleeves of her black sweatshirt like wings on her small frame. Even though she looked disheveled, she carried herself with rigid formality, as if she had decided that neither her past nor the present conditions of her life would determine her posture.

Oh marvelous, she trilled. How wonderful. So lovely.

I winced as she kissed Miriam on both cheeks, wondering where she'd picked up that particular affectation. Then she turned to me with a rapturous smile and opened her arms, standing on tiptoe to embrace me.

I'm so happy you're finally home, my love, she whispered. I missed you so much. My dear boy.

She held me close, her mouth hovering on my ear even after it was clear she had no more to say to me. I held my breath and waited for the moment to pass, and finally she let go.

My mother ushered us through the grand and drafty dining room and into the bright warmth of the kitchen, where there was food still set out on the table: a wilting, slimy salad; a haphazardly constructed cheese plate; half a torn baguette, its crumbs scattered over the soiled tablecloth; the picked-over carcass of a store-bought rotisserie chicken. A sextet of flies buzzed around us. The twins followed, making faces and snickering.

Oh darlings, have you *eaten*? Deedee gushed.

Please, please, you *must* have some wine! Kit sang.

Sweethearts, my mother interjected, shooing her daughters away. Don't worry, my dears. I'll take care of them.

She thrust tumblers into our hands and set plates in front of us. My sisters stood and stared, slack mouths twitching with mockery. I looked at Miriam, but she was handling the bombardment as well as she could, smiling politely and sipping the seven-dollar zinfandel that would stain her teeth and tongue.

Ma, I said. You don't have to.

Oh shush, of course I do.

Let the girls help you.

But they're so tired — it's past their normal bedtime.

It's not even ten.

Oh, well I just want them to relax and enjoy their big brother's company. It's been so long.

Then why don't they sit down with us

instead of watching us like we're zoo animals?

My sisters giggled shrilly and pulled up the chairs closest to Miriam, scooching themselves forward so that the chair legs scratched against the floor, their bodies jerking as if they were riding unbroken horses. My mother did another frenzied lap around the kitchen for no discernible purpose before finally sitting down herself to watch us eat.

So.

So?

Tell us everything. When is the wedding?

Ma!

I'm sorry, I'm sorry, I'm just excited to see you both.

Thank you so much for having us, Miriam said. We're so glad we could be here for your birthday.

Oh, I don't like to make a fuss of it, but it was a good excuse to have you come and visit. I was beginning to think that dear Thomas was keeping you from us, though I can't imagine why.

Ma.

She ignored me and began to pepper Miriam with questions she already knew the answers to — where she was from, how we had met, how long we'd been together. My sisters couldn't sit still. They kept getting up and circulating around the room, refilling their glasses with diet soda, bopping their heads, gyrating their hips, and humming along to music no one else could hear. They craned their necks to gape at the television mounted over the double sink, captivated by the lurid, ceaseless progression of bright lights and colors — pop stars pretending to be vampires, half-naked women writhing against sound equipment and palm trees.

And work? my mother asked, turning to me abruptly. Work is all right?

It's fine, I said. Busy since the promotion.

You never told me you got a promotion.

Yes I did, months ago. They're having me take the lead on some small campaigns. It's a lot more responsibility.

Well I'm sure you can manage it. We've always been so proud of you, my dear. Always taking care of us.

I felt light-headed. The food tasted strange, as if it had just turned the corner toward spoilage. I was afraid that Miriam would notice the skid marks of dried grease around the rims of the plates, the crusty residue at the bottom of our tumblers. I saw that her fork was dirty and took it from her, but before I could replace it my mother

39

snatched it away from me. She jumped up and went to the sink, ran the tap as hot as it would go, then returned with the newly shining utensil. She tittered under her breath about the dishwasher needing repairs.

It's because you load too much, Ma, I said, suddenly irritated. And because you don't rinse things before you put them in.

She laughed painfully. Don't be ridiculous, she said. I don't overload it. And you don't need to rinse things.

Yes you do, I said.

I don't think so.

It's fine, said Miriam. I'm finished eating anyway.

But you barely even ate, Deedee observed — the first words out of her mouth since we'd sat down.

Did you not like the food? Kit asked.

Girls, it's rude to notice what other people eat and don't eat, my mother said. Now please apologize to Miriam.

Oh, *Mommy.*

I mean it. Apologize now.

Sorry, Miriam.

Sorry.

It's all right.

I felt heat rise in my throat, felt an odd

40

prickling in my hands, as if they had fallen asleep.

Well then, my mother said brightly. Let's show you the rest of the house.

We all went back into the dining room, the floorboards banging beneath us. Miriam stopped to admire the painting over the sideboard — the portrait of a young girl in a sapphire dress, her gaunt face framed by lank curls, her shoulders and collarbone exposed. My mother noticed Miriam looking.

Ah, do you like our consumptive?

Consumptive?

Actually, we're not sure if she was consumptive, but she did have some kind of rare bone condition. See?

My mother pointed to where the bones of the girl's shoulders protruded unnaturally, hard lumps where they shouldn't be.

People usually think it's an amateurish painting, but that's actually what she looked like. She had some kind of disease that made her arms grow that way.

She died, like, the day after they finished the painting, Deedee stage-whispered, her eyes glittering as she squatted in an odd, graceless plié.

Not quite the day after. But soon after.

She died of a broken heart, Kit added,

41

grinning at Deedee.

Yeah, Deedee agreed, egging her sister on. She was, like, in love with the painter.

No she wasn't, my mother said.

They were supposed to run away together.

That's not true. She was only a young girl, like you.

But he never came for her.

No, he came for her, but then he left her there.

And when they found her the next morning she was dead and the bed was *covered* in blood!

You don't know that, dears, my mother admonished. And please don't be so ghastly.

How sad, Miriam said, trying to get us back on track. Who was she?

Some distant relative. We don't really know.

Dead, dead, dead, the girls chorused. Dead as dead can be.

Stop that now, please.

I had never liked the girl in the painting. She had stared at me all through my childhood like some kind of sick memento mori — a reproach to be good and eat one's vegetables. My father had called her his Little Mimi, after the tubercular heroine of *La Bohème,* his favorite opera. He had sometimes spoken directly to the painting when he wished to shame his two eldest children, refilling his glass and asking Little Mimi what she thought about our insolence and ingratitude as she gazed back at him impassively, Puccini thundering gruffly on the record player in the background. Evidently, the twins had their own strange associations with the portrait, though I couldn't fathom how those fantasies had developed.

We passed through the French doors to the double-height living room with the original fireplace and wrought iron balcony. There was a huge mirror above the mantel, hung just high enough that you couldn't see yourself in it, no matter where you stood. From there we went out to the screened sunroom, which opened onto the patio with the pool and the overgrown garden beyond, the fence keeping out the rustling of the tall hedges and towering pines. We took breaths of the night air before heading back inside. At some point we had lost the twins — bored by the tour and their own failed attempts to throw it off course, they had wandered away to some other part of the house without a good night or good-bye.

You have such a beautiful home, Miriam said.

My husband's grandfather built it in

43

nineteen twenty. It was his dream house.

It's very unique.

You can tell he was a bit of an eccentric — he came from a very *old* family. Doctors, mostly. Lots and lots of money.

It's like . . . Miriam paused, choosing her words carefully. Like an old house in a fairy tale.

There wasn't much around here back then. It was like living in the country. They had ten acres, all the way along the water-front.

How lovely.

Of course we had to sell all of that later — break it into parcels. Things could be tight sometimes when the children were young. Heating this place in the winter costs an absolute *fortune*.

Yes, I can imagine.

My parents had worked on and off throughout my childhood. There was money a long time ago — family money — and then it was gone. My mother had entered the marriage harboring the naive belief that she would never have to work, but by the time I was born my father had drained his trust and run his business into the ground, and my mother had purchased sensible heels and began to cycle through brief stints as secretary, administrative assistant, paralegal, and bank teller — anonymous office work that required no particular talent or skill other than the ability to get up each morning and snuff out any lingering spark of self-worth. My father attempted a number of similarly meaningless jobs, all the while raging against the system, his ill fortune, and above all his entrapment by his ungrateful wife and children. He had always been a drinker, and then he drank even more. Then he added pills, but he was always running out of those.

Through it all, my parents managed to hold on to the house, which had an elegance that I had always loved. Now that I was older, I felt real pain seeing it fall to pieces. I hated the peeling wallpaper, the angry scratches where furniture had rubbed, and the rot hidden under the paint. I wished it could look the way it was supposed to.

I noticed Miriam noticing the family photographs. She paused at the group portraits, and I could see her examining the children arranged in each frame — pallid figures faded from years of sunlight. I saw the questions forming, flickering behind her eyes.

Look, we're exhausted, I said quickly, laying my hand on Miriam's shoulder. I think we'll turn in early.

45

I wanted to pull my mother aside and ask about the ring, but I wouldn't have the chance that night. I had to get Miriam away, before she could ask about the photographs.

But I haven't even shown you the upstairs yet! my mother protested.

I'm sorry, I said. We just really need to sleep.

Miriam didn't question me — she never did. She took my hand and we said our good nights and went up to our room, the stairs grunting underfoot. We passed the second floor with its wide landing, the twins' room and my mother's room side by side at the far end of the hall. Then up to the third floor and down the long hallway with the worn, bloodred runner to the spare room, where the door had been painted over so many times it would only shut with a hard pull.

I lay down on the lumpy four-poster canopy bed without taking off my shoes and stared up at the oil painting on the wall, my eyes meeting the terrified golden gaze of a hart chased by a pair of hunting dogs.

They're sweet, Miriam said. Your family.

I turned over, away from her. The bedding smelled of dust and yeast.

What's wrong?

I don't want to talk about it.

I'm here with you, darling. I'm here to support you.

I said I don't want to talk about it.

She was silent for a while. Then she got up. I closed my eyes and listened to her moving around the room — hanging up her dress, putting things away. I opened my eyes a bit and watched the blurred shadow of her undressing — the rich cloud of her hair, the elegant scrolls of her shoulders.

Come here, I said.

I can't remember the exact details, but I'm sure we made love that night. We did most nights, sometimes more than once.

We probably played some game of Miriam's invention. She probably made up some story, slipping us into a fiction so that I wasn't sure what was real and what wasn't. Suddenly I would find myself in a different situation, with a different person, and I'd have to play along. But the basic outlines were always the same. She was wild, and I was wild for her. She was untamed, and I tamed her.

Maybe she mounted me, her hands on my shoulders. Maybe she told me about other men, her voice like slow honey. Maybe, as she moved against me, as she talked of others who'd had their way with her, she began to touch herself, her fingers tucked inside

47

her, moving in ways I couldn't see.

Maybe I grabbed her by her wrists. Maybe I rolled on top of her. Maybe I tapped my palm against her cheek, and maybe she spurred me on. Maybe I drew back and hit her face. Maybe she let out a hoarse bark that may have been a laugh. And maybe she placed my hands on her neck, tightening her fingers against my knuckles.

That's how it usually was. I'm sure that's how it went.

I do remember that later in the night, watching the dark blooms on her chest fade away, the blood draining back into the secret parts of her body, I turned out the light and she moved toward me, wedging herself under my arm. She whispered at my throat.

Thomas?

I was silent.

The other girl in the photos — is that your sister?

I pretended to be asleep.

Who was the other girl in the photos?

She was a diapered toddler on a beach. She was a lanky kid sitting on a rose-patterned sofa with two blond babies balanced in her lap, their heads like bright moons against her black velvet dress. She was a teen pirouetting on the front porch, her long hair a tattered banner behind her. She was a girl dozing in the grass with her younger brother, their arms arced carelessly over their heads, their upturned hands almost touching.

This was Eve. Our Evie. The photographs did not tell the story of who she was. They held no secrets or revelations; they were the same kinds of photographs that anyone would have. Even if they were saturated with the stink of tragedy, it was only in retrospect.

I'd told Miriam that I had an older sister, and that she had died. That was it.

This had been her bedroom. I pretended to be asleep because I didn't want to tell the rest of that story yet.

I still don't want to.

I must have fought someone in my dreams because I woke up with a start, sweaty sheets wrapped around me like a toga. It was still early, gray light pushing weakly against the dirty lace curtains. Miriam lay on the other side of the bed, her mole-speckled back turned to me.

But then I realized it wasn't a fight in a dream that had woken me. My throat ached and my eyes watered with the smell of something burning.

Downstairs, my sisters were peering into the oven. The kitchen was hazy with smoke — it hung on the shafts of morning light, made them solid.

The girls straightened when they noticed me, met me with startled, gray-toothed smiles. They both needed to see a dentist, badly. I pushed past them and turned off the oven.

What the hell are you doing?

We're baking something. For Mommy.

Since when do you bake?

Deedee shrugged. I looked up a recipe, she said.

We even followed it.

Mostly.

Well, whatever it was, you've ruined it, I said. I could smell it burning from upstairs. You'll have to throw it out.

Let us see it!

I opened the oven to show them the charred black lump inside.

You could have burned the house down, I said.

Kit crossed the room and roosted on the nest of newspapers that had accumulated on the window seat. She began to pick at a disturbingly large scab on her inner thigh, digging at the dark crust with her fingernail until it came loose and began to bleed.

Deedee said we should do something nice for Mommy, she muttered under her breath.

Don't sit like that, I said. Keep your legs closed and stop picking at yourself.

Make me.

Don't be a child. I have everything planned out. You don't need to do anything to help.

But we *wanted to.*

I had wanted to keep things simple. Bagels for breakfast, a nice dinner. If you kept things simple they were harder to ruin. Simple could be perfect.

Besides, it was just us, just the family — what was left of us. I had always hated how my mother poured her energy into elaborate productions for guests who never came. It was always disappointing. And now my sisters were acting out their own version of the same pathology.

If you want to do something nice then help me clean the kitchen, I said. This place is disgusting.

We just cleaned last week, Deedee said.

Two weeks ago, Kit clarified.

Well, look around! It's a fucking mess!

Don't yell at us, Thomas.

Doesn't it bother you to live in filth like this?

Suddenly I felt arms around my waist,

51

warmth at my back, Miriam's soft body pressing into my spine.

Oh my, she laughed. What happened here?

The girls stared at us for a moment, leering at Miriam's hands clasped over my navel, as if they'd never seen a healthy display of affection between two adults.

We tried to bake a cake, Kit said finally, chin raised in defiance. But we burned it.

And now Thomas is mad at us, Deedee added, smirking at me.

I'm not mad, I said quickly. I was just —

We can make another cake, Miriam said. Are there any eggs left?

I think so.

And butter?

Yeah.

Good. You'll help me, won't you?

My sisters nodded, suddenly docile.

Perfect. But let's clean first.

That's how Miriam was. She made everything better. Easier. She brought life and order to things in a way that I couldn't. She wasn't like other women I'd met in New York — the crazy and seductive ones. The ones who ordered round after round, the ones who made you meet them in bathrooms, the ones who swept you into cabs and laughingly bawled out the next destination — a bar, a hotel, her place, your place.

Those women would take control of you, but their good times were always on the verge of anarchy. They would say they needed you, they would beg you to stay. But when they were done with you, they'd drop you.

Even with her bedroom games, Miriam was different. Not at all frivolous. She made everything more enjoyable, more meaningful. You felt clean somehow, content in ways you'd never thought possible. Whenever she entered a room, she didn't just light it up. It was more than that. It suddenly felt as if her absence had been intolerable and unthinkable, her presence absolutely necessary. I could tell that my sisters were responding to her favorably, that soon they would adore her as much as I did.

An hour or so later, when my mother finally descended the stairs in her dressing gown, the smell of smoke was gone, the kitchen was clean, and the new cake was in the oven. My mother entered the room cautiously, wide-eyed, as if she were a guest in someone else's home.

Happy birthday, Mommy, my sisters droned, their voices oddly flat.

Look what we did.

Isn't it nice?

Very nice, my mother said, kissing each of

her daughters. Very nice. Thank you, my dears. You really shouldn't have.

She pretended to be happy, but I could tell by the shape of her mouth that her pleasure was tainted, that the sight of the clean kitchen had thrown her own negligence into relief — that our thoughtfulness was its own kind of rebuke. She looked around, perhaps noticing the rich peach color of the backsplash now that the tiles had been scrubbed of grime, or the way a brighter light hovered on the newly shining teakettle, or how spacious the counters seemed once they'd been cleared. Then she regarded each of us with a doubtful, close-lipped smile, as though she were trying to remember who we were.

We ate breakfast. We swam in the pool. Miriam wore a white bikini. I told myself to relax, that everything was fine. I told myself that I would find the ring.

But my sisters wouldn't leave Miriam alone. They complimented her ceaselessly and pestered her to smear sunscreen on their backs, leaning too sensuously into the caress of her palms when they easily could have taken care of each other without bothering her. They followed her from pool to chaise and back again, as if she were a toddler they couldn't let out of their sight, taking every opportunity to touch her bare skin.

Then they got bored with the pool and insisted Miriam come and see their art, tying towels around their waists and tugging her by the arm up the stairs. Their shared bedroom was a junk shop of porcelain dolls, stuffed animals, art supplies, and piles of clothing that must have dated back to the decade the house was built. They still had the same enchanted forest wallpaper they had picked out when they were six years old, wan fairies and spindly unicorns peering out at us from a gothic wilderness of elms. One wall had been swallowed up by a mural of the twins' own making — a thin, dark-haired girl with angel wings, suspended in a starry sky with the city at her feet. I averted my eyes when I realized who the angel was supposed to be.

My sisters dragged out their sketchbooks, their acrylics on wood panels, their oils on buckled canvases, and soon the bedroom was awash with young girls whose breasts and heads dissolved into butterflies or smoke, girls who were torn apart by flocks of outstretched hands, girls who sprouted tails and scales, girls who clawed their way out of gardens of succulents, girls who gazed into mirrors and saw monsters staring back, girls who embraced androgynous boys, their bodies bleeding together in swirls of shadow.

I leaned against the doorway while Miriam, still in her bikini, sat on one of the narrow beds and looked at everything my sisters showed her. She paged through their sketchbooks, letting her eyes linger on each work for the appropriate number of considerate seconds. She laid paintings down on the faded Persian rug, made a fuss over a few choice works.

I love this one, she said, examining an oil of an anemic couple floating together in a stormy sky. It reminds me of a Chagall. The colors and the gestures.

Oh, that's Bella and Edward, Kit said. From *Twilight.*

I'm not familiar, Miriam confessed.

You don't know *Twilight*? Seriously?

I'll explain, Kit sighed. So Edward is a vampire, but he won't drink Bella's blood because he loves her.

And he won't have sex with her either, Deedee added. Because he's afraid he'll kill her if he does.

I see, Miriam said, winking at me. How romantic.

They want to *so badly* though. It's insane.

56

Then when they finally do he knocks her unconscious and she gets pregnant but since it's a vampire baby it breaks all her bones and almost kills her and Edward has to, like, cut the baby out of her belly and finally turn Bella into a vampire.

You're too old for this garbage, I told the girls, but they ignored me.

They still didn't want to let Miriam go. They searched the room for other things to show her, rummaging through their belongings until Deedee opened a dresser drawer and let out a little gasp of delight.

Oh, Miriam! she cried. She held up a small battered box decorated with an evil eye. Can we read your tarot cards?

Miriam looked to me again, eyes mirthful, as if we were sharing a joke.

You don't have to, I said. Don't feel obligated.

Sure, she said, rolling the word over her lips. Why not?

This was how my sisters chose to spend their time. Tarot cards, horoscopes, natal charts. Slightly preferable to hours of television, on par with their overwrought art making, but not nearly as respectable as dipping their toes into the Western canon or hazarding some GED prep. They were very strange girls, would-be teenage witches, too old to act like such adolescents. And they were related to me. They arranged themselves with legs carelessly akimbo on the rug to begin the reading.

Okay, Deedee said. Miriam has to shuffle the deck first.

Miriam took the oversize cards in her hands and rearranged them, her long slender fingers transformed into crawling arachnids.

Okay, Deedee said. Now, think carefully about any questions you wish to ask the cards, and cut the deck for me. Choose five cards and lay them facedown in an arch. Like that. Exactly.

Just the five-card reading? Why don't you do Celtic cross?

It's too complicated. I forget what all the positions mean.

Deedee turned over the first card to reveal a woman in blue robes seated on a throne, a crown on her head, a scroll in her hands, and behind her, a veil of stars.

Uh-huh, Kit said, nodding to herself. That makes sense.

What? Miriam asked, looking puzzled.

So this first card is supposed to represent how you are at the present moment. And it's the High Priestess.

It means you're secretive and mysterious,

and you trust your instincts above all.

You're, like, typical High Priestess material. One hundred percent. Don't you think so, Thomas?

Secretive and mysterious? Perhaps. There were things about Miriam that I did not know, dark corners of her childhood and certain adventures from her years of travel that we hadn't yet explored together. But I knew she would tell me everything eventually. We could tell our stories slowly, judiciously, dealing cards from our decks and laying them on the table one by one. We had plenty of time.

So that's who you are right now, Deedee said. This next card is your present desires. The things that you want.

She turned over the card to reveal spears sailing through an open sky, their shafts budding with green leaves.

Eight of Wands.

What does this one mean?

It means you are moving with great haste and hope toward happiness.

You have a sense of urgency, but in a good way.

Miriam looked up at me and grinned.

Oh, she said lightly. I wonder what that could be about.

No idea, I said. Maybe you're going to

59

meet someone special soon.

Oh, Thomas, she sighed. Don't do that.

Just ignore him, Kit said. He's trying to ruin the atmosphere.

Now, Deedee continued. Here at the center we have the card that represents the idea of the unexpected in your life.

She turned over the card and nodded thoughtfully at the ivory hand clutching a crowned sword.

Ace of Swords. Very interesting.

Why interesting?

This is a very strong card, but it can represent force in both love and hatred.

Basically it symbolizes the triumph of something, but it could be either good or bad. So the fact that it represents the unexpected is interesting.

It's, like, double intense uncertainty.

I sighed audibly and my sisters glared at me. They wanted Miriam all to themselves, and I was ruining their fun.

Okay, what's the next card?

It was Adam and Eve, naked, flanked by trees of fruit and fire, gazing up at the terrible yet beatific visage of an angel.

The Lovers!

This is your immediate future. It means you'll find love and overcome your trials.

I'm sensing a pattern, Miriam laughed.

I'd begun to sweat. The air in the room had grown close, hot and humid from the wet bathing suits and the sticky warmth of bodies and breath. Somewhere outside a dog began to bark, and a lawn mower started up. Not in our yard, of course.

Yeah, sometimes it's like that, Kit said. Let's see what we have for outcome.

This is how things will end up for you, not just in the immediate future.

The card showed the great arc of a rainbow, a husband and wife holding each other close in rapture, two small children dancing beside them — seemingly oblivious, but apparently content. Beyond, a cozy house tucked into a copse of trees.

Ah, Ten of Cups.

That's a good one.

Classic happy-ending card.

This means you will have a perfect home and a good marriage.

All your dreams will come true.

I didn't realize the cards could be so clear about happy endings, Miriam said.

Sometimes it works out that way.

The happy ending was an appealing vindication, tempting to believe, but I didn't buy it. You couldn't put your trust in these kinds of things. You could try to convince yourself that the cards applied to your life and that they had special significance for you and you alone, but really everything was completely bland and generic. Any fool could see themselves in those stories, and any fool should be able to understand that promises of happy endings meant less than nothing. I looked up at the mural again and decided the angel didn't look like Evie at all.

Deedee collected the cards and had begun to shuffle them back together when Kit gasped and threw up her hands, almost striking Miriam in her panic.

Wait, Deedee!

What?

You didn't do it right!

What do you mean?

You read them all upright, but they mean different things when they're turned upside down.

Oh shit, you're right!

Like doesn't the Lovers mean the total opposite when it's facing the other way?

Was that one upside down?

I don't remember.

Don't worry, Miriam said. I'm sure it won't matter.

Of course it doesn't matter, I said. It's all nonsense.

Thomas!

You're rotting your brains with this stuff.

Stop ruining it!

I'd had enough. I stepped out into the cooler air of the hallway and crept carefully past my mother's darkened bedroom, where she'd been napping since breakfast. I hovered at the top of the stairs, waiting for Miriam to follow me, counting the long beats of silence until I heard the muffled, mouth-covered giggling of three girls.

I went downstairs alone.

I always considered Miriam to be an attractively rational person. She always expressed herself with cogent economy, never giving in to sulks or spasms of uncontrolled emotion. She was clear-eyed, almost cold in the way that she assessed every situation, gathering facts and proceeding with educated caution, with dignity, with regard for propriety and the feelings of everyone involved. She made lists of pros and cons, talked things through, never made important decisions without asking how I felt.

She was always so rational, and yet sometimes there were quiet glimmers of a sentimental nature that seemed to be at odds with what I knew of her. Secretly, when she thought no one was looking, she would get misty-eyed over the most absurd things, things she'd see online — a video about the plight of elderly shelter dogs, a news item about a man with a deteriorating brain whose stepdaughter asked him to adopt her, a car commercial depicting a family road trip to scatter the ashes of their dead patriarch into the Pacific.

Miriam would admit these moments of emotion to me later, laughing, as if she knew they were silly, but even as she tried to laugh it off her eyes would glaze over anew with fresh tears. And then I would worry she was too soft, too childlike, too much like the women of my blood.

Years later, I would wake and catch her praying one desolate winter night — hands clutching her elbows, body bent toward the frail glow of the ice-slicked bedroom window, her lips quivering with whispered words I did not understand. It reminded me of something I'd seen in an art history class, a painting of a girl reading a letter at an open window — weak sun on her profile, her somber face the only point of light in a darkened room.

I can't remember why she was praying. It's possible that I never asked her.

Late that afternoon I took my sisters in the car to go shopping. We needed to pick up a few more things for dinner that I hadn't had time to get in the city, and I figured it might be good for them to get out of the house for once and go for a drive.

Miriam stayed behind. I told her to relax and gather her strength for the evening ahead.

I regretted the excursion immediately. My sisters fought over the front seat, screeching and shoving each other out of the way like little children, then fought with me over the radio station, then fought with me again when I wouldn't stop at the ice cream parlor or the used clothing store on Main Street. At the Italian market in the next town over I ordered lamb chops from the butcher counter and the girls wandered through the aisles, shouting rude observations about what looked good and what didn't, fingering packages and produce. When I turned and saw Deedee lolling her tongue along an eggplant I chased them down.

Don't do that, I hissed.

Do what?

Touch everything!

Kit yawned and stretched the thin prongs of her arms skyward, revealing that beneath her oversize T-shirt she wasn't wearing any shorts, just the damp bikini bottom she hadn't bothered to change out of.

We're just seeing what they have.

65

Just checking out the wares.

You don't have to get your hands all over everything, I seethed. Not to mention *licking* a fucking *eggplant*!

Chill out, Thomas.

You're making people uncomfortable!

I think *you're* the one making people uncomfortable, Deedee retorted.

Yeah, can you keep it down? Kit hissed theatrically, lifting up her shirt and running her hands over her exposed ribs. You're kind of making a scene.

Deedee laughed, snorting loudly into her wrists.

It had been a mistake to bring them. A mistake not to buy all the food in the city. I grabbed a head of romaine and a quartet of beefsteak tomatoes.

We're leaving, I said. Let's go.

Why?

Because you embarrass me.

I felt ashamed as soon as we got in the steaming car. The girls both climbed into the back, took out their iPods, plugged in their pearly earbuds, and slouched in their seats, intent on tuning me out. I drove toward home, past the repeating pattern of pizza place, gas station, nail salon; pizza place, gas station, nail salon. We overtook a platoon of preseason cross-country runners

from the high school, the girls with swing-
ing ponytails, the boys shirtless, their chests
red and hairless. I could hear the tinny,
frantic beat of my sisters' music, the distant
sound of wailing.

This wasn't me. I was the good older
brother, the role model, the nurturer, the
protector. I was here to help my sisters, not
antagonize them. Clearly they needed all
the help I could provide. They'd always
looked up to me, had always loved me —
clambering into my lap, drawing pictures
for me, somersaulting on the lawn to show
off (*Thomas, watch me! Watch me! Watch
me, Thomas!*), hungry for the affection that
I gladly gave. I was the doting father that
none of us had ever had.

As we were about to reach our street, I
had an idea. I drove past the turn and kept
going until we saw signs for the Ocean
Parkway.

Just a quick ride, I murmured to myself.

The girls looked up briefly, registering
without comment that I had decided not to
take us home. Soon we were trundling over
the bridge, the choppy blue bay beneath us.
Once I turned on the radio and let the girls
pick the station, they finally began to relax.
They rolled down the windows and loosened their topknots and let the faded, gem-

streaked strands of their long hair whip around their heads. They stretched their bare, sun-slashed limbs. Ocean air thundered through the windows, vibrations pounding in our chests.

Finally I saw the exit for the beach we used to visit when we were children. Most cars were leaving for the day, a halting herd moving back onto the parkway, their windshields blinding pentagons in the lowering light. I eased into the parking lot and found a spot close to the rail, where we could see the grassy-haired mounds of the dunes, the sandy spread of the beach, and the blue of the water beyond. I cut the engine, rested my hand on the back of the passenger seat, and turned to regard the girls.

Listen. I'm sorry about how I behaved just now.

They looked at me wordlessly, their eyes vacant. I took a breath.

I'm not going to make excuses, I said. I just get frustrated sometimes because I just — I just want the best for you.

They were listening carefully now, leaning toward me, not a trace of boredom or mockery on their faces. They knew that what I had to say was important. Smart girls, they had always been smart girls, even if they were a little strange. I felt sure they would understand what I had to say next.

I want to talk about a plan, I said.

Now they looked at me blankly. The moment went on a long time, until Kit finally broke the silence.

What plan?

You know, I said.

Uh, no, we don't know.

Just — a plan! I said, exasperated all over again. A plan for your lives!

Oh, *that,* Deedee sighed.

Yeah, *that,* I said. Have you thought about school?

Kit scoffed, as if she were choking.

Moving out? I tried. Getting your own place together?

Really, Thomas?

What?

You really have no idea.

What do you mean? Don't you want something else out of your lives?

They had slumped away from me again, their arms crossed protectively over their chests.

It doesn't matter what we want, Deedee said. It's just not going to happen. It's impossible. There's no way we can leave that house.

You can still apply to college. It's not too late for that. If I could do it, so can you.

But you could only do it because Mommy let you.

We didn't even finish high school.

Finish high school, then, at least. You can take classes online.

Mommy doesn't want us to.

She doesn't own you.

But she takes care of us.

You're old enough to take care of yourselves.

No we're not.

You are.

Mommy says we're not.

She doesn't want to lose us. Like she lost Evie.

We were silent. Our sister's name hung between us as the light in the car grew more and more golden, immolating our faces.

What if I talked to her? I said finally, shielding my eyes from the sun's glare. To Ma.

Good luck with that.

I'm serious, I said. I'll talk to her. But only if you really want me to.

It's not going to make a difference, Kit sighed. Trust me.

And then I knew that they didn't want it enough. They were satisfied to stay as they were, to stay in that house as our mother's little girls, safe and secure in their enclo-sures.

We didn't talk for a while. We looked out at the beach, watching slow waves roll in to shore, watching the small dark silhouettes of families packing up to go home. The girls hadn't even asked if we could get out of the car. I put it in reverse and joined the depart-ing herd.

I like Miri, Deedee said suddenly.

Yeah, Kit said. I do too.

Miriam, I said, bristling at the overfamil-iarity of the nickname. Her name is Mir-iam.

She said we could call her Miri.

When did she say that?

I guess you weren't there, Deedee said.

We were silent for a few moments. Then Kit took a breath. Are you in love? she asked, pulling herself forward, her hands on my headrest, her voice soft with reverence.

Yeah, Deedee chimed in, hopeful, trying to catch my eye. Are you going to marry her?

For once they weren't making a disgust-ing joke out of love — for once, they weren't trying to turn it into something foul. I swal-lowed my annoyance at their effrontery and allowed myself to grin at them in the rear-view mirror.

Maybe, I said, winking. I just might.

Good.

They settled back into their seats, seemingly satisfied, closed their eyes, and let the breeze run its fingers over their faces as I drove us home.

When we got back Miriam and my mother were sitting together in the sunroom, tea gone cold in their cups. They fell quiet when they saw me approach, looked up with sly grins, as if they'd been caught misbehaving.

How was the shopping?

Fine.

Your mother and I have had such a nice time chatting.

So she hadn't rested, like I had suggested. Instead, she'd been subjected to hours of my mother's prattle. I had no idea what they might have talked about. I couldn't even begin to guess.

Miriam and my sisters went upstairs to change for dinner. I lowered myself into a wicker rocking chair and looked at my mother, who had stretched out on the love-seat, her bare legs mottled and mapped with veins. She had picked up a worn paperback copy of *Ordeal by Innocence* and was paging through it, pretending to read. I cleared my throat.

Did you have a nice afternoon?

Mm-hmm, she said distractedly. Lovely afternoon. Miriam is lovely.

What did you two talk about?

She turned a few more pages of her book, as if she hadn't heard me, as if I weren't even there. I felt a familiar dizzy panic rising in me, the feeling that things were not under control. She could have told Miriam anything. I forced the words out again.

What did you talk about?

Oh, nothing really, she said. Nothing important.

I sighed, gathering myself.

What's happening here? I asked.

My mother looked up finally, confused and hurt, as if I'd insulted her.

What do you mean?

What's going on with the girls?

She rose and began to move around the room, her hands fluttering awkwardly as she tidied up.

They're fine, she murmured to herself. They're completely fine.

Fine? Are you crazy?

What do you mean?

Just look at them, Ma. Do they seem fine to you?

Look, Thomas, we hardly ever see you, she said, turning to face me. You can't just come here when the spirit moves you and then get angry when things aren't up to your standards.

It's not about my standards! It's about the girls.

They're perfectly happy.

What about school? Or jobs?

She made a vague gesture, as if she were shooing something away.

Ma, they have to do something.

They will, she said. They're still so young. I'm letting them focus on their art.

Jesus, Ma. That's not going to get them anywhere.

Not everyone needs to *get somewhere.* You've always been in such a rush, and it's never helped you.

Ma, don't.

You wanted to do everything right away, even though everyone told you it was more important to do well than to do it quickly.

This isn't about me.

You took on too much that first semester, two labs and your job and everything. I knew if you had just —

This isn't about me!

Dinner at last. A fist-sized hole had rusted through the bottom of the grill, so I seared the chops on the stove, then carried them out to the glass-topped table on the patio.

74

Miriam had already set out the snacks I'd brought from the city — olives like emerald birds' eggs, truffled goat cheese wrapped in brown paper, pink sausages dotted with fennel seeds — and my sisters had descended on the spread, ravenous. They ate the skin of the sausage, the part you were supposed to peel away, and hooked their fingers into the cheese, licking its thick cream off their cuticles and wiping their hands on the once-white mildewed petticoat slips they'd decided to wear as party dresses. My mother splashed wine into huge, smudged crystal goblets, her bony wrist arched ostentatiously. We cut into our lamb and it was an impeccable medium rare.

The pool lights had been turned on, the water like a phosphorescent lake beside us, punctured by the dark circle of an inner tube. The sun had set, the lower edge of the sky pale blue against the black fur of the softly breathing hedges. My mother leaned back in her chair, let her gaze swoop up to the last blush-colored streaks high above us.

Perfect, she said. Everything is perfect.

She looked at Miriam across the table.

When I was a girl I never imagined I would live in a house like this, one day.

Miriam nodded in encouragement, her eyes locked on my mother's. She loved to

75

hear other people talk about their lives.

I didn't grow up poor, exactly, my mother continued. We always had everything we needed — enough to eat, new shoes every year and all that. But I was definitely used to a more humble sort of life.

She wasn't being completely honest. My mother's family had been quite poor — her father had died young, and her mother had raised five children on her own. She had often been hungry, and always had to work.

I was seventeen when I met Thomas's father, she continued. He had just graduated from college. Amherst. His family belonged to the yacht club, and one day he wrote his phone number on the little slip for their charge account and handed it to me as I was clearing their lunch dishes.

Another lie. After my father died and before I went away to college, my mother called me to her room one night and made me lie down in bed beside her and told me the real story of how they had met. At the yacht club, yes, but after midnight at the annual Fourth of July party, when my father stole into the kitchen to slip a hand up my mother's skirt and fold her like a dish towel over the industrial sink where she'd been washing wineglasses, telling her over and over again that he knew she had wanted it like this for a long time. She had mistaken his aggression for passion, and after that had allowed him to do what he liked, whenever he liked. She began to seek him out, longing for the intensity of his attentions. No one had ever bothered to notice her like that before.

We had such a ball that summer, my mother told Miriam. He had his own car, and we'd drive around and go to the movies and the beach and do other things like that. One time we took the ferry over to Fire Island — he had some friends in Saltaire who let us stay over. And of course he paid for everything. Dinners, little gifts. All the time.

Everyone likes to say that nineteen sixty-three was the last summer of innocence for people like us — you know, white and middle class — but I think that's being too generous, she said. It was even worse than what people say. I had no idea what was happening in the rest of the country — you couldn't have paid me to read a newspaper. I cared about my hair, and what I wore. I'm ashamed to admit it now, but it's true. We were in our own little bubble, and we stayed in that bubble for a long time, even when the rest of the world began to change.

All right, I murmured, not liking where

this was going. It's all right, Ma.

We got married that winter, my mother continued. We had said we would wait until I finished high school, but we had a courthouse ceremony around Christmas. People thought I was pregnant, but I wasn't! We were just tired of not being together.

She wouldn't say it, but the truth was that he had been jealous. He was afraid of losing her to someone else — filled with rage at the thought that some other man would take what was his. And so he insisted that they get married, before my mother could change her mind.

He promised that our marriage would be different from other people's, she said. He promised we wouldn't settle into the same old awful routine of brisket and briefcase. He told me it would be a great adventure. And for a while it really was! We traveled all over, went to the opera all the time. I never had to do my own laundry. Everything was perfect.

She left out the other features of their marriage, the other routines that developed almost immediately: the confrontations over phone calls from unknown women (her tearful entreaties, his denials and counter-accusations), the fights over spending money that quickly turned into perverse games of slaps, the nights he came home and slept belly-up in the foyer because he was too wasted to climb the stairs, the nights he failed to come home at all.

It sounds like a very happy time, Miriam said.

Oh, it was, my mother said. She hesitated, but only for a moment.

Things changed after a few years, she went on. They changed for everyone in the world, of course. But for us too.

Ma, I said, a warning in my voice. She ignored me.

We were in San Juan. The water was so blue. We were staying in the most charming hotel in the old part of town. Everything should have been wonderful. But my husband was upset that week. He could be very moody sometimes — without any warning, usually. He'd had a very easy life for the most part, and when anything went wrong he just couldn't roll with the punches, you know?

One night we were having dinner on the beach and he told me that he had regrets. He was scared of the future — he'd gone into business with a friend, and it wasn't going well — and he wasn't sure if he was meant to be married or have a family. He thought he didn't deserve that kind of happiness. Which isn't true, of course. Everyone deserves to be happy. But he could be very sad sometimes.

Mercifully, she let the story end there. She didn't tell Miriam what that night had really been like, or what had actually happened — how totally obliterated my father had been, how he had screamed at my mother for ruining his life and struck her across the face in front of everyone in the restaurant, how he had stalked off and slept alone on the beach that night.

And she didn't explain that the only reason he didn't leave her was that, after years of trying and four miscarriages, she was finally pregnant.

It was a good life, though, my mother said. When the children were little we used to camp out here some nights. There were so many stars — he taught them the names of all the constellations, told them all the stories behind them.

She trailed off and looked away, and I followed her gaze, watching the fleeting green throbs of fireflies pulse brightly before fading back into the dark shadows of the garden.

But why am I saying all this? my mother asked, remembering herself. Don't listen to me, I'm just rambling about things that no one cares about.

That's not true! Miriam protested. I care.
I'm *very* interested.

Oh, you're very kind, my mother said. But
really it's all very boring. The kids have
heard these stories millions of times and
they don't want to hear it all again.

Deedee and Kit nodded vigorously.

We want to know more about *you,* Miri.

Miriam laughed softly, the lens of everyone's attention focusing on her. She wel-
comed their gaze — she must have sensed
that I desperately wanted to change the
subject.

What do you want to know?

Everything.

Why did you leave Paris?

She shrugged. I wanted to see more of the
world. And then I met your brother.

She touched my hand, applied a compan-
ionable pressure.

But aside from all that, it's not the best
place to be a Jewish girl who looks like an
Arab.

Really? Why not?

People can be nasty about it.

How?

They call you names. Sometimes they follow you on the street. Things like that.

My mother put down her fork, blinking

and then widening her eyes to emphasize that she was listening closely.

Did anything bad ever happen to you?

Not really. Well, actually, there was the one thing. When I was a little girl.

What happened?

Tell us!

I was abducted.

She said it so casually, as if she had told the story many times, even though I had never heard it before. My sisters leaned forward with open mouths.

Oh my god.

That's *crazy.*

Don't be so panicked, Miriam laughed, waving her hand like a bored dauphine. It was only for a night. I didn't even realize at the time that I had been abducted.

You have to tell us the whole story, said Kit, clutching her paper napkin.

All right, all right, Miriam said, sitting up slightly, laying her palms on the cloudy pebbled glass of the tabletop. I think I was six, maybe seven. I was walking home from school, and the woman who lived down our street was out in front of her house. I remember she was wearing a long skirt that was sewn together from all these colorful patches, like something a gypsy would wear. She called to me, and when I approached her she told me that my mother had asked her to take care of me for the afternoon. She told me I had better come in for my goûter.

I don't know what that is, Deedee said.

Oh, a goûter — it's a snack. All French children have it after school. Anyway, no one had warned me about going into strangers' houses, especially if it was a woman who invited you in — I thought all women were mothers, and that meant they were safe. I trusted this woman instinctively, because I had no reason not to, so I followed her inside.

Oh dear, my mother said.

How stupid of me, eh? But I didn't think twice. The woman served me chocolate and bread, and then she let me watch television, which I never got to do at home. There was a cartoon about a spoiled princess courted by a dozen different princes, and a movie about a unicorn transformed into a white-haired maiden, and of course *Babar.* I must have watched for hours, because eventually it got dark, and the woman said I was supposed to stay over for the night, and that my parents knew I was safe with her. For dinner we ate pasta. It was all very nice.

After dinner the woman sat me back down in the living room and told me that I was the prettiest little girl she'd ever seen. She asked me if I'd like to eat chocolate and pasta and watch television every day, and I said that sounded very nice, but I wondered if my parents would be all right with it. The woman told me not to worry, that my parents knew all about it, but that there was one thing they didn't know.

What?

They didn't know that I was going to hell.

My mother put her hand over her mouth.

Oh, *Miri,* Kit breathed. She had begun tearing her napkin into little pieces, rolling the bits into tiny balls with her fingertips. She popped one into her mouth and sucked on it noisily.

The woman told me that all Jewish children went to hell when they died, Miriam went on. And in hell they wandered alone in fire and darkness, and would never find their families again. It wasn't their fault, of course, but they were damned because their parents didn't know any better. They didn't know what to do to save them.

Oh my god!

At this point, I was beginning to get a little frightened, as you can probably imagine — but the woman took my hands and said that *she* could save me, that she would make sure that I went to heaven like all the other good children. She wanted to do it for me, because I was the prettiest girl she'd ever seen, and she knew I deserved it. All I had to do was trust her. So she led me into the bathroom and asked me to take off my clothes while she filled the tub.

Holy shit.

Did she, like, *touch* you or anything like that?

Did she *molest* you?

Sweethearts! That's inappropriate!

No, Miriam said. There was nothing like that. She had me get in the tub, and she put her hand on my back, and said a lot of prayers asking God to protect me, and suddenly she had her other hand on my forehead and was pushing me down under the water.

No way! Deedee gasped. Did you fight back?

No, because I trusted her! Miriam said. It sounds crazy, but I really did! I thought all adults took care of children, and that their job was to keep us safe. They were our protectors, you know?

In any case, I wasn't afraid. I lay there on my back, and after a moment the woman lifted me up out of the water. When I opened my eyes she was smiling and crying and saying that I had been saved.

I can't believe this, Deedee said. This sounds like a movie.

Yeah, a really fucked-up one, Kit agreed.

Then she brought me into the bedroom and gave me a man's shirt to wear as pajamas, and we lay down together in the bed. She told me that now I was a child of God, and that I was truly perfect, and that someday I would go to heaven where I belonged. Then she told me to go to sleep, and that we'd make plans in the morning.

Plans for what? Deedee asked.

Miriam shrugged.

It never got that far, she murmured. She was quiet for a moment, her eyes lowered to her plate. A stillness settled on the table — even the breeze had died.

The police arrived a few hours later, Miriam continued, looking up at us again. Two officers. One of them called my parents from the phone on the bedside table. I could hear my mother wailing on the other end.

Wow, Kit whispered.

What happened to the woman? Deedee asked.

You know, I really have no idea, said Miriam, her voice light and wondering. I never saw her again. I heard her crying somewhere as the police led me out of the house.

God, Kit murmured. I can't believe this.

You know, said Miriam, I think maybe she wanted a child of her own but couldn't have one for some reason. So she tried to steal me and convert me.

You think so?

I mean, it was ridiculous, really, Miriam said, leaning back in her chair, her neck long and white. I can't imagine she thought she'd succeed in keeping me permanently. Maybe she only wanted to pretend, to see what it was like for a while. I can understand it. The wanting to pretend. I've done that too.

You have?

Well, nothing as crazy as that, of course.

I stared at Miriam, imagining that strange house, furnishing it with views stolen from the homes of strangers and acquaintances, places visited once or twice and barely remembered: a dim sunken living room, beige carpeted stairs, floral curtains, a chipped blue bathtub. A small girl in a huge bed, cradled in the arms of a barren woman who was making plans for heaven. It was like something out of a horror movie, and I should have put my arm around Miriam and pulled her close to me, drawing her away from that awful memory.

But I didn't.

You never told me that story, I said. She met my gaze and shrugged.

It never came up.

I had always wanted to know about her, had always hungered after the secrets of her early life, but now I had the carcass splayed before me, and I felt sick from watching the others gnaw at the bones.

My own traumas were more than enough to sate me — we didn't need hers.

My sisters had left the table without my noticing. They reappeared as shadows at the threshold of the sunroom, a garland of fire hovering above their outstretched hands. Everyone began to sing.

After the cake, my mother thanked us for the lovely evening and went up to bed. I could tell she was holding back tears by the way she pressed her lips together, her chin crinkled as if it had been smashed into gravel.

Everyone else would have left the dishes until the morning, so I cleaned up the kitchen alone, scraping clods of confetti frosting into the trash and rinsing every knife, fork, and plate before loading them into the dishwasher. I shut the door and pressed the start button, listened as the meek hum of the machine filled the silent room. Everything had been put away.

When I went back outside I could tell the

girls were drunk. All three of them. They had descended from the table to sprawl out carelessly on the patio, their eyes shining with something besides the electric blue light of the pool, their laughter and voices loud enough for the neighbors to hear. My sisters were telling stories to Miriam, who leaned toward them, transfixed, prodding them with her nods and her questions. At first I could only make out isolated snatches of their talk, but as I drew closer, their words began to cohere into a familiar, shameful narrative. Then I was standing beside them, witness to the confessions I was powerless to stop.

And people just didn't believe us, Deedee was saying. One day in kindergarten I told everyone that Daddy had hit Thomas with a frying pan, and they all laughed.

Well, Kit said, that's because it was kind of funny.

I guess so.

I mean, it sounds funny to a little kid. Getting hit with a frying pan.

They thought I was making it up. It just sounded so crazy.

Kit put her face in her hands, her body convulsing with what looked like sobs. She couldn't get her words out, couldn't breathe.

But she wasn't crying. She was laughing.

Remember? she finally choked out.

What? Deedee asked. What?

Remember the night Thomas threw Daddy down the stairs?

Now they were both laughing, bawling with hysteria. Miriam stared at them as if she were dazed.

Don't tell that story, I said. But they didn't hear me.

Daddy was so drunk, Deedee said. Thomas didn't even really need to push him.

He missed the step and — *whoosh!*

Like he was on a slide.

And *boom* at the bottom.

Didn't he sleep there all night?

No, Thomas dragged him out to the porch, remember?

Evie helped him. It was right before she left home.

They went quiet then, suddenly remembering themselves, remembering what they weren't supposed to talk about. They looked up at me, and in the cringe of their bodies and the glossy darkness of their wide eyes I saw what I must have looked like to them — I saw that they were afraid of me.

But Miriam didn't shrink away, or shut down. Instead she drew closer to my sisters, embracing them with her gaze and her touch. Soon the three of them were kneading each other's shoulders, caressing each other's ankles, joined in a feminine circle of comfort. I half expected them to kiss.

Tell me about Evie, Miriam said. I've always wanted to know more about her.

She was the best.

But she lied about everything.

Everything!

She told people she'd run away from home when she was thirteen.

Or that our parents were dead and she took care of us.

Or that she was going to be on the next season of *90210.*

Or that she was having an affair with her English teacher.

They were smiling again, relishing these memories.

What happened to her? Miriam asked, her voice low.

She moved to the city for college. She lived on the sixth floor.

And one day she fell.

No one spoke after that. We listened to the sounds of the pool and the sounds of the night — the burbling of the filter, the hiss of the crickets, the brackish breeze that rose up and fidgeted through the greenery.

■ ■ ■ ■

There were things my sisters didn't know about Evie.

They didn't know that we would hide in her bedroom and read, just the two of us. They didn't know about our pretending at love, or that when we tired of our mother's romance novels we would read *Where the Red Fern Grows,* returning again and again to the scene where the boy dies, impaled by his own ax in the Ozark night, the red bubble forming and breaking on his lips.

They didn't notice how Evie arranged puzzle-piece bits of food in colorful symmetry on her plates, how she would tongue teaspoons of soup like a kitten, how she needed something green on every dish, or how she ripped up her bread with her fingernails until it disappeared.

They didn't know about the bright dashes of sharkskin on her upper arms, tidy marks like a growth chart.

And they didn't know about the other things that had happened. They hadn't even been born yet.

I can still see myself, nine years old, walking home from the park where I've gone to kill time after school until my mother comes home from work. I kick up leaves and caress rows of hedges with my outstretched hand. I pass a dead squirrel, ironed into the road like a dried flower pressed between the pages of a heavy book. I crunch up the driveway, tiny gravel fireworks exploding from under my footsteps, my plaid shirt coming untucked, my jacket slipping from my shoulders.

Inside, the lights are out. But then I hear Mimi, our father's favorite: *I came happily from my little nest, to respond to your call of love.*

I float through the vestibule, through the dining room, drawn toward the music, toward the presence emanating from the living room like a smell.

It's my father. Facedown on the couch, spotlit by a single dim lamp, he props himself up on his elbows and looks at me with glazed eyes. He opens his mouth slightly but no sound comes out. Mimi and Rodolfo are singing together now, reluctantly bidding their dreams of love goodbye before agreeing to stay together until spring. *To be alone in winter is a deathly thing.*

And then I see Evie. She is asleep, maybe — her eyes closed, her body still, so thin you can hardly see her there, under our father.

She is thirteen.

My father tries to wink at me, tries to turn on his trademark sparkle, but his eyes are red and slow. From where I stand I can smell his pickled breath.

I panic. I know it's absolutely essential to keep my mother away from that room, because if she found our father and Evie like that, found the three of us there together, something terrible would happen. I know that I have to protect my mother from that scene, even if I can't protect my sister.

Marcello and Musetta are quarrelling now, their volleyed accusations a vicious counterpoint to Mimi and Rodolfo's reconciliation. I begin to cry. My father is crying too and he gets up and screams at me to go outside, his voice joined with the shouted crescendo of Marcello's and Musetta's bitter insults. I don't move — I can't move — and my father steps forward and hits me across my face.

Then I'm on my back on the floor, the wind knocked out of me. My father grabs me and slings me over his shoulder and carries me outside, then goes back in and slams the door behind him, Evie in there with him, Mimi and Rodolfo on the stereo singing together as one:

We'll part when it's the season for flowers again.

After a while I stop crying. I sit on the porch until it gets dark, until my mother comes home from whatever office she's indentured to that year. I watch her get out of the car and waddle up to me. She is hugely pregnant, exhausted, the twins huddled together inside her. She smiles at me, her dear boy.

They kicked a lot today, she says, taking my hand and bringing it to her belly.

She doesn't ask me why I'm outside. I don't tell her anything.

You wouldn't have believed our father was capable of such things. To an outsider, he seemed devoted. And even though Evie and I knew the truth, the apologies were always so lavish, his amnesia concerning specifics always so total, that we almost wouldn't believe it ourselves.

Later that night, Evie crawled into my bed with me and held my hands and whispered that it hadn't been so bad, that he'd only wanted to lie there on top of her, looking at her.

I let myself believe her.

The twins also didn't tell the story of how it all ended, years later. How on the fifth day of one of his benders, my mother let our father bully her into giving him the car keys so that he could drive himself to the deli at the end of the street.

She must have been worn down from the days of delusional rants, the months of overdraft notices. She must have been tired of living in his world, where facts changed because he said so, where everyone was always out to get you. The world where you could hit your son with a frying pan, because no one would stop you.

Besides, the deli was only a few blocks away.

Ignoring the stop sign, our father coasted through the intersection, and the oncoming Volvo station wagon plowed through his driver's side door, flattening my father into a slab of jelly and gristle.

The other driver was a high school softball star, had pitched her team to the state championship that year. She would never walk again, but she survived. Things could have been much worse. If my mother ever felt guilty about what else might have happened, she never let on.

After the funeral — smug relatives and gawkers from the Methodist church descending on the house to gorge themselves on cold cuts and baby carrots, rainbow cookies wet with jam — my mother found me lying on my back in the garden grass, the sacred space where my sisters would chant incantations and cast spells. She pulled my head into her lap and stroked my hair. She was drunk, half laughing, half crying.

Man of the house, she kept murmuring. Man of the house.

It was just after sunset, and the mosquitoes had grown bulbous and brave. My dark blazer was spread under me like a cape, already stained beyond mending.

In my mind I can see my mother taking off her ring and hurling it into the dark wall of the hedge, but I know I'm imagining that.

I was seventeen. The twins were almost eight. Evie had just turned twenty-one.

We should have been fine afterward, our entire lives ahead of us. Instead, Evie was dead by Christmas, and the twins stayed home, little girls forever. Now that my mother could finally protect her two youngest, they would start all over again from the beginning, two babies safe under their mother's watchful care.

I was the only one who managed to escape.

Don't mistake me. I'm not looking for sympathy. That's the last thing I want.

■ ■ ■ ■

I climbed the stairs to my mother's room. I knew she wouldn't be asleep — she could never sleep at night. She'd be up reading, or watching an old movie on the small television she'd set up on her vanity, or gazing at the faded roses blooming on the walls.

I knocked softly, entered. My mother was sitting up in bed, pillows in mismatched floral linens piled around her, light from the television dabbed against her shabby nightshirt. I caught a glimpse of the screen, watched two sisters singing and dancing in the parlor of a grand house. The elder sister was a famous starlet — she would die of an overdose one day.

Sorry to disturb you, I said.

It's all right. I'm sorry I missed the rest of the party.

No, it's good that you left when you did. The girls embarrassed themselves.

Oh.

She didn't ask me how — she could probably guess. She cleared her throat. They shouldn't drink at all, she said. It's my fault — I don't know why I let them.

Ma, they're twenty, for Christ's sake. It's fine.

Let's please not have this fight again, she said.

But Ma.

What?

This isn't what I want for you, I said. You shouldn't be living like this.

Thomas.

I can help. I can take care of the girls. And you.

You do take care of us, my love.

Of course I do. I always will.

You're so much better than your father ever was.

Just tell me what you need.

She was silent for a while, and when she looked up again her eyes were dull, defeated.

We need money, she said. Her voice was like the thud of a hand on a table, a door pushed shut.

That's fine, I said quickly. That's totally fine. I can give you money. It's no problem. Everything will get better.

She wouldn't look at me. We said nothing, listening to the bright babble of the voices coming from the television.

If you like-a me
like I like-a you
and we like-a both the same
I like-a say this very day

99

I like-a change your name
'cause I love-a you
and love-a you true
and if you-a love-a me
one live as two
two live as one
under the bamboo tree

Where is your ring? I asked, breaking the silence.

What ring?

Your engagement ring.

Oh.

She got out of bed and crossed the room to her dresser, opened the top drawer and peered in, sifting through the drifts of threadbare underwear. Without looking at me, she extended her arm and handed me a small box, its black velvet partly worn away. Inside there was a subtle gleam, like an eye opening in a dark room.

I thought maybe you'd thrown it away, I said.

Of course not, she replied. I would never.

She began to move around the room, tidying the piles of old magazines and cast-off clothes, talking quickly.

It was supposed to be for Eve. You're supposed to give these things to your oldest girl — I always meant for her to have it, when she grew up. But you — you take it. It should be yours now. Miriam is a lovely girl. I'm very happy. Very, very happy.

Don't cry, Ma. Please.

She turned away so that I couldn't see her face.

My sisters were back in the pool — naked this time, though I had begged them to put their suits back on — carousing and calling out to each other like a pair of naiads. Miriam and I sat on the edge with our legs dangling into the water. Our limbs were pale and green — they looked as if they didn't belong to us. She swirled her left foot in slow circles, brushing it against mine.

I'm sorry, I said.

Why are you sorry?

This wasn't what I wanted it to be.

What do you mean?

I didn't answer. We watched my sisters for a while — their bodies alien and elongated, their features lost to the ripples of the water. They floated on their backs and looked up at the stars.

I just want to do it all the right way, I sighed finally. Love and family, everything.

We will, darling, Miriam said. We'll do it the right way.

I want us to have everything I never had, I

101

said. I want to build a shell around us so that we'll be protected.

She took my hand then, and I knew how it all would be.

I could see us back in the city, holding hands at a table after a waiter had collected our menus, leaning our heads together as our train rumbled through the darkness under the river.

I could see us meeting with an immigration lawyer downtown. We'd open a joint bank account, get Miriam's name on my lease. I could see the dossier of snapshots and correspondence that we'd amass: the evidence of our life together, of our love. I could see Miriam in white on the steps of city hall. My wife.

And I could see her holding a squirming bundle, sitting in the leather club chair in our living room, milk spilled on her wrist like a cuff of lace. I could see private school, a cubby labeled with a musical name, a child carving out the letters of the alphabet with a crayon clutched in a sticky fist.

Now I can see that Miriam wanted to protect me just as much as I wanted to protect her. We were two of a kind, my wife and I. If my life up to that point had been like an old and battered house, she wanted to rip the rot from the rooms, banish the bad memories, throw open the windows, and fill the place with light and air and the breath of the future.

She loved me very much. She did.

I didn't propose that night. I wouldn't for another two weeks. But that night I could see myself kneeling before Miriam with my mother's ring. I could hear the promises I'd make about the life we'd have, my words alighting on her — on us — in fully formed perfection, as if in a dream.

I could see how I would keep her.

II

I once read an article online about a polar bear in a zoo that ate its own cubs.

This kind of infanticide had been seen in the wild before. Up in the Arctic, a group of scientists had sighted an adult polar bear devouring the bloody carcass of a cub, the small body so mauled that it was initially mistaken for a seal. Climatologists and other experts said this behavior was on the rise. Driven to desperation by ever-shrinking ice, the famished bears were turning to their own young as a food source, killing them with sharp bites to the head, the same way they would kill a seal, as if there were no difference between their children and their prey.

But this news story was different. Determined not to raise a pair of soft, dependent polar bears, the zoo staff had refused to hand-rear the babies, even when it became obvious that their mother couldn't care for them. Better to let nature take its course and let them starve than interfere, the zoo said. Let wild things stay wild, even as we charge admission for you to see them, print their faces on T-shirts, sell their likeness as stuffed animals.

The staff thought everything was going fine. There'd been no crying from the cubs, which seemed to suggest they were well fed and content. But when they finally entered the polar bear's cave they found no sign of them, and their mother was no longer hungry.

In the uproar that followed, experts speculated that the mother might have seen the cubs as a threat, or that the stress of captivity may have driven her to filicide. But I think she may have done it to save her children — to save herself. Her cubs were extraneous. They could bring her no joy or satisfaction, and she knew she couldn't care for them. She had failed as a mother.

The story reminded me of *Medea*. I have always loved the 1959 Maria Callas recording at Covent Garden, when she was both in her vocal prime and at the pinnacle of her artistic maturity. She is radiant in that last scene, debating with herself, agonizing over what it means to be truly merciful. Leave her beloved children in the care of their vile and traitorous father, or do the business fate has given her?

So it must have been with the mother bear, exerting her terrible love the only way she knew how. Better to kill her young than to see them waste away in that dismal cave. Better to draw them back into her, where they could be at peace.

Then again, they were just animals. It's not as if they act rationally. They don't know what it means to be heartless.

Let's move ahead now.

Picture me a decade and change gone by. At forty-two, I still have all my hair — or almost all of it. These days it leaps back a bit from my temples, as if recoiling in surprise, but it's just as lush as ever on top. I have only the slightest, softest smudges of silver in my day-old stubble. I own four blue suits and three gray suits, a khaki suit, and a seersucker suit, but today I'm in jeans and a navy linen blazer, brown leather loafers, and a white oxford shirt.

It is early October, and it is unseasonably mild, as it usually is these days in autumn. The sky aches blue. The fiery foliage crackles. It is the Friday before Columbus Day weekend, and today I'm not at the office — where I've ascended from junior art director to senior art director to associate creative director — because as soon as school lets out we're driving up to the Berkshires to visit our friends for the long weekend (big house, five wooded acres, good wine, a fireplace). And because I'm not at the office, and because Miriam is out buying car snacks and housewarming gifts, and bringing the dog to the kennel and running other last-minute errands, and because I've been on call all morning with my team running through their preliminary, unsatisfactory ideas for the new AiOn smartphone campaign pitch — because of these things, I'm the one who answers our home phone when it rings just before noon. And because I answer the phone, I'm the one who makes the twenty-minute drive east along the Long Island Sound to the Anne Hutchinson Academy for Girls — or Hutch, as the students call it — where my daughter has recently started sixth grade.

Now picture me pulling up to the campus in my iridium silver Mercedes S-Class sedan and parking in the visitors' lot, Renée Fleming cut off mid-vibrato as I kill the ignition. Picture me ambling through an Arcadian fortress of redbrick Georgian cottages, over grounds crisscrossed by slate paths and sheltered by regal oaks. Hutch was originally founded as a boarding school for the daughters of aristocrats, and there was a time when each girl would arrive in September with her own maid and horse. One can still spot the occasional wandering deer.

Picture me walking alone down a cool, dim hallway lined with lockers, the student body safely sequestered behind the closed doors of their classrooms, and picture me ushered into the hushed sanctuary of the headmistress's office. Picture me seated in a tufted leather chair, tapping my foot against the polished floor. Picture the rich mahogany shelves filled with books, the rainbow of alarmist spine copy — *Conversations with Ophelia, Guiding Our Daughters, The Crisis of Adolescence, Lilith Speaks, Whatever Happened to My Little Girl?* Picture the art on the walls — pink-fleshed mother and child by Cassatt, pensive portraits of important women. Picture the lovingly illustrated Welsh alphabet that lines the upper perimeter of the room, the curious letters illustrated by sweet little sheep and cheerful boats. Picture the homemade ceramics on the broad gleaming desk, and picture the woman sitting behind that desk. Dark skin, curly hair tamed into a tight chignon. She's pushing fifty, I think, but then again, it's hard to tell with black women. In pearls and practical gray suit, she projects an aura of serene authority. Only the fleck of plum-colored lipstick on her front tooth mars the effect. This is Dr. Alice Hanover, Head-mistress. She has a laptop in front of her, and on that laptop are screenshots of a sugar baby dating profile supposedly cre-ated by my daughter — the reason for today's little tête-à-tête. Dr. Hanover has thus far managed to avoid showing me what is on her screen, but she is talking quite a lot.

Now that you see everything, let's listen in.

As I'm sure you can understand, we take these matters very seriously, especially with our middle school girls. They're at such a vulnerable point in their development, and we find these types of incidents can signal real problems with their self-esteem. This behavior is a major threat to their well-being and the well-being of their peers, and there's just no place for it in our community.

Now, I'm sure she didn't mean any harm. She's been very adamant about the fact that creating the profile was meant to be a joke, and that she and her friends were only hav-ing fun — but as I'm sure you know, girls this age often don't understand that their actions have consequences. Serious consequences. And it's particularly serious in this instance, because your daughter is such a leader in her cohort, and she inspired other girls to get involved, and now their images are out there too.

I wondered about this Dr. Hanover. She'd been headmistress of Hutch since my daughter entered first grade, but I'd never bothered to meet her, or read her biographical blurb in the school newsletter. I left those kinds of details to Miriam, who would occasionally fill me in on what she thought I should know.

I knew that Dr. Hanover was a Hutch alum, and that she'd gone to Smith, then Harvard for her PhD. I imagined she'd harbored dreams of being a star academic — perhaps art history, or Romance languages and literature — but in the end she had returned to manage the halls she'd walked as a child. For someone ambitious, it must have been a disappointment, a step down in prestige. Then again, judging from the tuition we paid, her compensation had to be considerable.

I recall that the hiring of the first black headmistress at Hutch had been a big deal. Many pats on the back had gone around, talk of the school moving into the twenty-first century. Diversity, representation, inclusion. But then some parents began to complain quietly that there was a certain aloofness, even a chilliness to Dr. Hanover's demeanor. They allowed that she was lovely, and perfectly poised, but they felt that she didn't quite fit with the culture of the school, or its traditions. They said she could be hard on the girls.

That was what Miriam had reported to me, anyway.

Now, these images are just the ones that have been saved, Dr. Hanover was saying. Apparently the girls posted similar content on some other apps — you know, the ones that delete almost immediately. We have some screenshots of those, but not the full-length videos. I'm sure you know how difficult it is to keep up with the new technologies — ideally we'd issue a new code of conduct every month! In any case, the girls just don't appreciate that other people can see these things, and that once it's out there, they can't take it back.

We'd really stretched ourselves to secure my daughter a place at Hutch, and I was beginning to have second thoughts. I'd wanted her to have a classical education, but for some reason it had taken until fifth grade for her to master long division. The school had no standardized curriculum, and the quality of the faculty was incredibly inconsistent. Some of the fresh-faced shepherds in the lower school didn't even have teaching degrees, and in the upper school they were either former PhD candidates who'd never finished their dissertations or weary veterans of the public school system. Hutch marketed itself as a haven for girls who were passionate about learning, but the students seemed to care about the wrong things, obsessing over their penmanship and the strict color-coding of their notes. According to Miriam, the mothers formed cabals; they cast appraising eyes over the make and model of other girls' sneakers and backpacks, whispered about standardized test scores and tutors. Privately, I often worried that my wife was excluded from these small-minded centers of social power because of her foreignness, her Jewishness. Stranded in an insipid sea of white Protestants, she simply failed to fit in. No one had ever said anything to her directly, of course.

And aside from my doubts about the school's rigor and culture, its financial difficulties seemed to be mounting. They were starting to sell off some of the property near the water to pad their endowment, and soon there would be luxury homes along the soccer field. Each year's tuition bill was higher than the last, the semiannual fund-raising letters increasingly plaintive.

I'm sure you had no idea this was going on, Dr. Hanover was saying. We don't blame you, of course. We don't blame anyone. We know she made a mistake — and she's deeply regretful. But she needs to learn what's appropriate and what's not. And she needs to learn how to protect herself. Because these issues will only deepen as she gets older. Better she absorbs these lessons now, before anyone gets seriously hurt.

I'd thought anything had to be better than public school. Even though everyone said the public schools on the North Shore were much better than the ones I'd attended, I still shuddered to think of those fluorescent-lit linoleum penitentiaries, remembering their particular humiliations. In elementary school I was reprimanded for reading ahead, nauseated by the ever-present smells of urine and old milk. High school had been a cheerless stockyard overseen by security guards in black polyester jumpsuits who were never quick enough to stop kids from vaulting over cafeteria tables to throttle each other. In other ways, it was a lawless place: cigarettes sucked hungrily in the bathrooms, covert blow jobs executed in the stairwells.

As far as I could recall, no actual education had taken place.

I'd wanted something different for my daughter, never mind the social challenges or the expense. Wouldn't you have chosen the same?

At least she was learning Latin.

She's a lovely, lovely girl — all her teachers say she's an absolute pleasure to have in class. I know she's genuinely sorry, and our top priority is to keep her on the right track. Now, I know you must have questions —

May I see the profile now?

As I said before, Mr. Martin, I do believe it would be best for you to examine it with Mrs. Martin, in the privacy of —

Please let me see it now.

Dr. Hanover hesitated, then turned the laptop around and clicked on an image to enlarge. There was my daughter in an unspeakable state, shielding the shameful parts of her body with a strategically positioned homemade sign: BAD GIRL.

I couldn't believe what I was seeing. I looked away before the details of the image could fully register. I shook my head, opened my mouth and closed it again.

I'm sorry, Dr. Hanover said. I know it's shocking to see it — I'll admit I was completely shocked myself. I wouldn't have expected this kind of behavior from her, but I must say again that most of the time when a girl acts out like this, it's an expression of some deeper troubles. A cry for help, as they say. She may benefit from talking to a therapist, and we are more than happy to recommend —

Is she suspended? I asked abruptly.

Dr. Hanover blinked once and pursed her lips.

No, she's not suspended, she said. But I think it would be best if she goes home for today. She was very, very upset when I spoke to her, and I think she needs some time for reflection. I'm sure you'll want to have a family discussion rather soon — I'm sending you these files now, so that Mrs. Martin can see them — and as part of that discussion I recommend setting boundaries for social media use without making it into a forbidden fruit. Above all, it will be important to foster a culture of conversation so that she feels comfortable coming to you with questions in the future. Always begin by listening.

With that, she extended her hand for me to shake. Her palm was cool and dry, her grip firm. She nodded, smiling with sober eyes.

Thank you so much for coming in.

The meeting was over, and I'd barely gotten a word in. Had I allowed it to happen? Had I let this woman boss me around and tell me how to raise my daughter? Had I let the serene, invisible mechanism of authority bulldoze me into silence? Why hadn't I fought back and told her that I would handle things my own way? Was I that much of a pushover?

No, I decided. That couldn't be it. I was just too much of a gentleman to interrupt or protest. Let this middling bureaucrat believe she'd had her way. My daughter was still mine. I was in control.

And when I stepped out of the office, my irritation melted away into a sense of quiet resolve, because there she was. At some point while I was in there being lectured she'd sat down to wait in the vestibule, her long legs and gangly body nearly swallowed by the enormous leather sofa she had slouched into. She was dressed in her uniform, khaki pleated skirt and crimson polo, too old now for the garnet plaid pinafores we'd always adored. Her left knee was skinned from last week's soccer game, and she was still tan from the summer. She looked up from her cell phone, which she wasn't supposed to be using in school, shook her dark hair out of her limpid brown eyes, and met my gaze, her face grim.

My daughter, my Ava.

First there were the Polaroids. Miriam had shoe boxes filled with them — white-framed, washed-out totems from those first years of courtship and marriage. There I am at an outdoor café, bright sun erasing the crown of my head, my shoulder, my wrists. There I am commandeering the grill, smoke like a spirit beside me as I scowl manfully. There we are on the steps of city hall on a gorgeous autumn afternoon, Miriam ducking from the hail of rice thrown by our friends, holding up her bouquet as a shield as I turn toward her, my palm open to catch the celebratory hail.

There we are in photo after photo, self-portraits with our faces pressed together, missing pieces of her forehead, or my chin — one eye, one mouth. There we are at someone else's wedding, my right hand reaching across my body to hold her arm above her elbow, her right hand twined with my left. There she is with a hand cradling her swollen belly, her other hand brushing back her hair, or wiping her brow, or shielding her face. There we are standing together in the gravel driveway of our life-size white dollhouse, closing documents and keys in

117

hand, grinning like fools.

And there is a parcel of pink on a powder blue bedspread: short chubby legs, feet kicked aloft to touch a tiny chin. A little body on its back, pulled into the shape it must have held in the womb.

Then things go digital, and I mostly disappear. Scroll through the albums that first year of my daughter's life and it's all mother and child. Miriam smiling in oversize sunglasses, pale baby flesh pressed to her chest. Close-up of Miriam gazing into the lens, lips puckered to kiss the sliver of baby profile peeking out of a blanket. Baby's head resting against her mother's knees in a hammock, pedicured feet stretching up toward a cloudless summer sky. The photographs suggest a never-ending idyll: every hour magic hour, every bottle-feeding and bath and bedtime a work of art.

The reality was somewhat different.

Miriam's parents were the first problem. They didn't bother to come to the wedding — they saw no point in dragging themselves across the Atlantic for a civil ceremony — but Miriam prevailed upon them to visit that December, her first Chanukah away from home.

Their taxi pulled up just before sundown.

From our front door, we could see their dour faces peering out at the street, as if they were afraid to leave the car. Miriam's mother was a small and elegant woman, her thick dark hair shot through with white; she said very little, communicating through endless touches on her daughter's arms and shoulders. Her father was neatly dressed, reserved and unsmiling. He shook my hand firmly, and I met his eyes for a full three beats before he looked away.

I tried to curry favor over dinner as I told them about the house we would buy very soon, my upcoming promotion and raise. They nodded distractedly as Miriam babbled in a torrent of French and English, translating furiously, until her father sighed and held up his hand.

I understand, he said, his voice clipped. He was just too proud to answer me in English that was anything less than flawless.

They were obviously not happy. They'd expected their daughter to come home, or at least marry a Jew. They couldn't fathom her life in New York, or understand why she'd chosen me. After dinner Miriam's mother lit the menorah and the family chanted hymns I did not know.

Throughout the week they were in town, I hardly saw them. Miriam took them to museums and other places of interest during the day while I was at the office; the first few nights they came back to the apartment to have dinner and light the candles, but toward the end of the trip they elected to stay in their hotel in the evenings.

I confess they remain somewhat gray to me, these characters that entered our married life so briefly. Promises were made about having a real Jewish wedding in Paris the following summer, promises that were not kept. There would be no long family vacations, no affectionate favors performed for my mother-in-law, no intimacies shared over late-night glasses of scotch with my father-in-law. I never became their son; I can barely recall the particularities of their faces.

When I think of that visit, I mostly think of Miriam's anxious expression, her eyes flitting back and forth between her parents and me, her husband, as she recognized the sundering between her old life and her new one. I felt a palpable sense of relief when these strangers finally went home, leaving my wife and me alone together.

Her parents may have been the first imperfection in our fairy tale, but as soon as Miriam got pregnant we relapsed into bliss. I always thought it was a cliché to say that women glow when they're expecting — and I'm sure that for most women, it's not true at all — but Miriam really did glow. She gave off this warmth, this light, even more so than she usually did. I wanted her all the time, even as her body became strange and unrecognizable to me, with its swollen breasts and new growths of hair. It excited me to think that I was responsible for changing her, that I was the one who had altered her body so markedly.

I only have one bad memory from those months. It was early summer, her second trimester. We were still living in Brooklyn, and I was coming home from work, ambling through the warm violet evening down corridors of sturdy townhouses occupied by prosperous families. I turned our corner and saw her down the block. She was in a cornflower blue maternity dress, facing away from the street, looking into someone else's garden. Miri, my wife. I came up behind her and put my hand on her elbow, and when she turned I saw that she was smoking a cigarette. It trembled in her fingers for a brief moment before I knocked it out of her hand.

What are you doing? I said. She took a step back from me.

I'm sorry.

Are you crazy?

I said I'm sorry!

I knew we were making a scene, right there on our pleasant street, and the shame of the spectacle inflamed me further.

How could you?

I needed one, she said. Just one.

You *needed* one?

I couldn't help it, I'm just so, so —

She couldn't finish her sentence. She began to cry, and after a few moments of watching her thin frame heave with sobs, I folded her into my arms, the gentle mound of our baby pressed against me.

It's okay, I said. I forgive you.

That was when I decided it was time to get serious about buying a house, as I had promised Miriam's parents. The apartment was barely big enough for the two of us, and it was time to start living like adults. Like a family. House hunting would give us a project, a constructive outlet for Miriam's anxiety, which was beginning to mount. She refused to buy anything for the baby or do more than the bare minimum of research, citing superstitions, the evil eye, other nonsense.

A house would be different. A home was something to look forward to.

We'd gone to a few open houses out on Long Island earlier that spring, just to get a feel for the market, but now I kicked the search into high gear, broker and all, and we spent the summer scouring the hamlets of the North Shore.

Finally, on a warm Sunday in September, we pulled up to 26 Harbor Lane, a Dutch Colonial with a wide porch and dormer windows, half an hour northwest of the house where I'd grown up. Golden light soaked the lush lawn. Looking at the house, I could imagine the sound of footsteps and happy shouts, could see first-day-of-school photos taken on the porch, trick-or-treaters congregating in the doorway, Christmas lights strung up in the towering apple tree in the front yard. I could smell Miriam's cooking in the renovated open kitchen, feel the warmth of fires I'd build in the living room hearth. I could see a life lived — our life.

Miriam needed a little more persuasion. She'd gone along gamely with the search, but when it was time to make an offer she balked. She wasn't ready to abandon the idea of a larger place in Brooklyn, even though I'd told her again and again that with our budget those kinds of places didn't exist, and that staying in the city wouldn't make sense for us in the long run. Still, she resisted. It was her trust fund, and the down payment on the house would eat up most of the principal, leaving us house poor aside from my income. But it was what we wanted. She kept asking if we were sure, and I kept reminding her yes, of course we were sure.

We closed in early November, a few weeks before Miriam's due date, and after leaving the lawyer's office we stopped by the house that was finally ours, just the two of us. In the front vestibule I popped open a bottle of celebratory champagne, the cork bouncing away from me into the dark and empty living room, ricocheting off the wall.

To us, I said, raising my plastic cup.

To us, Miriam repeated.

She took one sip, then poured the contents of her cup into mine.

Miriam had hoped her mother would come back to New York for the birth, but in the end she couldn't. I can't remember why. It may have been prohibitively expensive, or perhaps her husband didn't allow her to. Her mother's absence caused my wife some distress; at the hospital, there was much more crying than you may have expected, even considering the challenges of the delivery. Four hours of pushing before they finally cut her open. The bleeding would last for days.

But all the pain was worth it. I would give anything to go back to the beginning and see myself holding my daughter for the first time. To see the excess ink of her footprint pressed to the back of my hand, to see those glittering eyes staring into mine, even though their memory scorches me now. That first moment, holding her — everything they say about it is true.

We named her Ava, for my sister.

We went home, I went back to work, and before we knew it, winter had descended on us. I had imagined that we would settle into comfortable domesticity relatively quickly, but things didn't work out that way. Months after we'd moved into the house, the floors were still bare, artwork was still unhung, and cardboard boxes still cowered in the corners of the rooms. My mother and the twins didn't come by as often as I'd thought they would — the girls were obsessed with the new baby, but they still couldn't drive back then, and after the first few visits my mother was less and less inclined to leave the house and brave the traffic on the park-way.

Other kinds of disorder crept in. I'd come home from work just after seven and see the breakfast dishes still on the counter — yellow slick of egg dried to ochre, curls of desiccated orange peels. Miriam would be on the sofa, the down comforter from our bed tented over her. The television was always on, always set to some costume drama — intrigue among the servants, grand balls, pale-skinned aristocrats delivering restrained professions of love.

I called my mother.

You need to come over more often, I said. Miriam needs company.

She doesn't want me there, Thomas.

What do you mean she doesn't want you?

When I call to invite myself she makes all sorts of excuses about why I shouldn't come. I think she just wants to be alone.

Well, that's too bad! It's not her decision.

You try telling her that. I don't want to be where I'm not wanted.

I started to notice that Miriam only held the baby when she absolutely had to, laying her back in her crib as soon as she was done feeding. When Ava cried, Miriam would sit impassively and wait for several seconds of squalling before shaking herself out of her reverie and going to get her.

One evening over dinner — leftover rotisserie chicken, frozen spinach that had been indifferently sautéed — things finally came to a head. I'd turned on the radio to a broadcast of *Così Fan Tutte* — one of Mozart's lighter confections, a farce about conniving fiancés that we had always enjoyed. Miriam must have asked me how my day was, because I launched into a monologue about some of my recent frustrations, particularly the bovine inflexibility and lack of imagination in management.

They want it every which way, but it's completely vague, I said. Their imagination is only quantitative — it's all about how much money they can wring out of people. It drives me absolutely insane.

I attacked the remains of my chicken breast, chewed and swallowed the dry meat.

But they can't actually do anything to hurt me, I said. They know I'm not disposable. And that's the good news, really. This kind of creative work is never going to go away. It will be a long time before machines can generate original ideas. Although I guess you never know these days.

I had been talking like this for a while before I noticed Miriam wasn't listening to a word I was saying. She hadn't eaten anything; she stared at her untouched plate as if it were a text she didn't know how to read. Her eyes bulged with unshed tears. Her lips shuddered.

Miri?

Suddenly I noticed how disheveled she looked. She'd been wearing the same dull blue cardigan for days, its sleeves falling to her knuckles, hiding her engagement ring. Her hair was lank from a week without washing, and a cluster of pimples climbed her neck like a grapevine. Her breath smelled like sour beer, and her face was swollen and pink. She was hunched over, shoulders curled in, neck bowed and tense. It wasn't like her to sit like that. It was as if she weren't embodying herself as the woman I knew.

Miri? Sweetheart?

It was intermission. The host was talking softly, crediting the leads and conductor as recorded applause faded in the background.

Miriam opened her mouth to speak.

Why did we move here?

At first I didn't know how to respond. I didn't know what she was asking.

What do you mean? I asked finally. We wanted this house, remember? We never would have been able to afford this much space in Brooklyn. You know that.

But we don't know anyone here.

We have my family, I said. They're not far.

But we don't have any friends.

Our friends aren't in the city anymore either! I said, showing my exasperation more than I had meant to. They're all in fucking Jersey, or Westchester or wherever!

Don't yell at me!

Sorry, I said. I'm sorry, sweetheart. I didn't mean to yell.

She closed her eyes, swaying slightly in her chair. When she finally spoke again her voice seemed to come from very far away.

I can't stop thinking about it.

What?

Don't be angry with me.

What can't you stop thinking about?

Please don't be angry.

Tell me.

I can't stop thinking about hurting her.

We were silent for a long moment. On the radio someone was droning on about a membership drive, warning listeners it was their last chance to give.

Miri, I said, nearly choking on her name.

She looked down at her hands, refusing to meet my gaze.

Miri, I repeated.

Every time I hold her, these awful visions come into my mind, she said. I think of how easy it would be to open the refrigerator and leave her inside, or fill the tub and slide her in. Or, I don't know, just drop her. She's so fragile, she would just break.

The clarity of these visions startled me. It was as if someone else were speaking through my wife — my small, sweet wife who could never hurt a living thing, who could never harbor such thoughts.

Whenever I look at the top of her head and see that pulse beating I just imagine crushing it with my fingers.

She had begun to cry. I grabbed her wrists.

Miri, Miriam! Listen to yourself!

It's like it's not even her, she sobbed. I look at her, and I don't know who she is. Or what she is. I keep dreaming that I go to the crib and she's turned into a bird, or a swarm of bugs. She's not my baby.

She is your baby, I said. She's our baby.

I'm so sorry. I don't want to hurt her. I just can't stop thinking about it. I want to kill myself. I want to die.

No you don't.

Yes I do.

Don't say that. You don't mean that.

She squirmed in my grasp, trying to free herself, but I held on, even as she dragged our fused hands through her uneaten food.

I can't do this. I can't be her mother. I don't want to touch her. If I touch her I'll hurt her.

130

No, you're a perfect mother. You're not going to hurt her. You just need help. We'll get help for you.

I keep hearing noises in the house. I keep thinking there's someone else in here.

There's no one else, sweetheart. I promise.

You don't understand. You aren't here. You don't know what it's like. All I do is wait for you to come home. That's all I do. Every day.

You need company. Ma and the twins, they can come over —

I don't want them. They're weird — they're not my family.

Miri, come on.

Just let go of me! Let go!

She was howling, making animal sounds. I'd never seen her like this before — never seen her dissolve so completely. It scared me. It made me see her differently, showing me a capacity for darkness that I had never believed could exist in her. I let go of her hands.

Now, of course, I hate myself for ignoring her loneliness. There was so much that I didn't see — that I refused to see.

Ava was wailing too now. I went upstairs to her room and gathered my daughter in my arms, came down and paced the living room with her, singing softly even as her mother continued to moan, a song about two people who promised to be together forever despite the trials they would face, despite the unforgiving passage of time.

You and I, together forever, I whispered. You and I.

When I moved back toward the table Miriam left her chair and staggered upstairs into our bedroom, where she collapsed facedown onto the unmade bed. I followed her, still carrying Ava.

Look, I said to Miriam. Look. She's perfect. She's perfect and she's ours.

Don't bring her near me. Take her away.

No. I want you to see her.

I don't want to!

I lay down beside Miriam, balancing Ava on my chest. I began to coo to her, my daughter.

Mommy loves you. She's scared right now, but she loves you.

Miriam shuddered beside us, her back turned.

Everything is going to be okay, I promise.

We lay like that for a long while, until Ava's wet breaths grew slow and even against my throat. I carried her back to her room and set her down in her crib, then returned to our bedroom. I lay down again next to Miriam and wrapped my arms around her, trying to hold her quivering body still.

I know it's hard right now, I said into her ear. I promise nothing will ever be this hard again.

Up to that point, our life together had been safe and warm, the doors of our happiness sealed against the world outside. But now a draft had forced its way in, the first dissipation of ease, of security, of perfection. For the first time in my married life, I felt threatened by something I could not control. It didn't matter that I had a good job, or that I had secured us a home. I saw that my girls were vulnerable to mysterious and external forces, forces that could destroy us if I wasn't careful.

But I was stronger than the threat. I scheduled an appointment for Miriam the next morning, and the doctor put her on medication immediately. I made other changes. I put more work into the house on the weekends, so that it finally felt like home. I began to take night duty almost every night, waking up to cradle and feed Ava, soothing her when she cried. Sometimes I'd take her downstairs, and we'd fall asleep in front of the television, the damp ballast of my daughter against my breast. Other nights, when she wouldn't settle, I'd walk around with her, whispering.

This is your room, I'd say. This is your crib, and these are your books, and these are your toys. This is the hallway. That's Mommy and Daddy's room. This is a window. Out there is our street. There's the tree you'll climb when you're older. I'll show you how.

Day by day, life regained its idyllic glow, the photographs no longer falsehoods as the years went by. There they are, my girls, sitting on our front stoop in matching sundresses. There they are in the backyard, tanned arms slung around a homely curly-haired mutt — our dog, Beau. There they are in the pool at my mother's house. There they are in cream-colored sweaters, gazing up in open-mouthed awe at a glowing Christmas tree. There they are in red velvet seats at little Ava's first opera, my girl yawning widely before the second act of Engelbert Humperdinck's *Hansel and Gretel.* There they are at a picnic table, Beau at their feet, the heavy shadows of an overhead trellis falling in dark bars against them.

I must have taken most of the photographs. That's why I'm not in them. We must have asked someone to take that family portrait on the beach at sunset. I must have given my phone to some stranger to capture our joy, allowing another person into our intimate orbit for just a moment.

No. That couldn't be it. Looking at it again, I can tell I must have taken the photograph myself, that I must have stretched my right hand as far away and above as I could to keep us all together in the frame.

We would never have looked that happy — that open — for anyone else.

When my daughter was born, I was stunned by the realization that she was mine. First it had been just my wife and me, and suddenly there was another person in the room with us — a new presence that had come from us.

She hadn't come from my body as directly as she had from her mother's, but when I held her I could feel the ways that she was part of me. We breathed together, her small being swaddled by my chest and arms.

The epiphanies only accelerated as she grew. There — the infant rolling herself over — she's a part of me. There — the toddler with the dark curls reaching for my hand, pronouncing her first words — me. There — the girl reading chapter books on her own — me. I was reminded afresh each day that she was an individual, a separate person, but part of me still. I could remember her at every size, the different ways she used to fit against my chest and lap, how she slowly grew away from my body's walls and corners. A small and perfect satellite.

I can still see her now. Not just her face, her gestures too — all those little idiosyncratic movements that made her. They come over me like a wave.

Ava never had to try to make friends. From the first day of preschool, other children were drawn to her dark prettiness, her impish smile. But there was something else about her. She didn't throw tantrums. She didn't show need. She'd always been self-assured. *Let them come to me* — she seemed to know this intuitively. And she was magnetic. Even as children, we are helplessly drawn to the ones who don't need us.

She wanted to be popular, and she was. Adored by her peers, she was invited to every party, never excluded or shunned. She dispensed hugs with deft efficiency, decorated birthday cards with intricate designs in rainbow gel pens, posted effusively captioned photos of herself with her friends:

ilu
bff

soooo happy we're friends
u are flawless
ugh so freaking cute
omg adorable
princess
slay queen
xoxo

She ruled over her cohort as a benevolent empress, deciding when and how they would coordinate hairstyles, which teachers they liked and didn't like, which foods they would deign to eat, which topics they would gossip about over lunch, and whether boys as a concept were cute or gross in a given week. Her amiable exterior masked an unshakable sense of self-confidence, a conviction that she was the starlet in the movie of her own life. We could see it at home sometimes in the way she'd disregard us if she didn't care to hear what we were saying. She wasn't rude about it — she'd just tune us out, turning her face, letting her eyes drift to something else in the room. Like an icy society matron, intent on keeping up appearances, even as she froze you out.

I'm *thinking,* she'd retort when we pressed her to answer us. Or she'd just change the subject and babble on about something else.

That was the Ava I knew: self-assured, unflappable. My own little Princess Turandot, that imperious beauty and executioner of unworthy suitors — though my daughter was more real and dear to me than any Puccini heroine.

Now, banished from school for her scandalous act, my daughter's cool-girl facade was crumbling before my eyes. She ran on ahead of me toward the parking lot, her hands pressed to her reddening face as she dodged a posse of older girls on their way to lunch, squealing in exasperation as she found the passenger door locked. Finally, safe inside the Mercedes, she slumped in her seat and sobbed, all her careful polish melting to reveal an uglier, more vulnerable core.

Ava, I said sternly. Listen to me.

She cried harder, mashing her pretty face against her knuckles.

Get ahold of yourself.

I can't.

You have to stop crying and listen to me.

I can't.

How could you do this? How could you?

I didn't mean to do it! I didn't mean to! It was just a stupid *joke!*

She wept bitterly, spitting her words. The hair around her cheeks and brow frizzed

138

with the hot moisture of her face.

You're crying like this because you don't want to take responsibility! You need to stop it, right now!

She began to gasp, over and over again, and suddenly I thought of my father, of Evie — suddenly, I was afraid that my daughter would seize up and stop breathing, and that it would be all my fault.

Sweetheart, don't, I said. Please don't. You'll make yourself sick.

I laid my hand on her back, and she took a few deep inhales, the bones of her shoulders rising and falling against my palm.

It's okay, I said. It's okay. Calm down.

Now you won't love me anymore, she whimpered.

What?

You and Mommy, she said, turning to give me a baleful look. You won't love me because of what I did.

Of course we still love you. But you made a very big mistake.

Don't tell Mommy. I don't want her to know what I did.

I have to, sweetheart.

Please don't tell her. *Please.* She's going to be so angry at me.

The real problem, I knew, was that my wife wouldn't be angry enough. Her natural inclination was to smooth over conflict with affection. Though she could be strict about quotidian, inconsequential matters — like Ava wearing a coat in cold weather, or eating everything on her dinner plate — when it came to big-picture issues Miriam could be hands off to the point of neglect, saying Ava should be free to make and learn from her own mistakes. Apparently that was how they parented in France.

That wasn't the way I parented, especially not in a situation this serious, when there was no room for such maddening inconsistency. Now that my daughter was no longer in hysterics, I knew I had to get through to her and make her understand the gravity of what she'd done. I had to take control before my wife had a chance to undercut me and kiss it all away.

Listen, I said, my hand resting on the back of my daughter's neck. Let's go for a drive, okay? We don't have to go home yet.

Aren't we going up to the country house? Ava asked, skeptical.

Not until later, I said. We have time to kill.

Where are we going to drive?

Where do you want to drive? We can go wherever you'd like.

I don't know.

She had taken out her phone again — last year's AiOn, with the bigger screen and better camera, a relentlessly begged-for birthday present — and was scrolling through something, her half-closed eyes glazed by the diamond light of the screen. She sighed heavily.

What? I asked. What's wrong?

One of the Kitty Angel's baby kittens is sick.

What?

The Kitty Angel. She rescues tiny baby kittens when they're, like, only a few days old and takes care of them until they're old enough to be adopted.

She held up her phone so that I could see the photo: a buxom, heavily tattooed redhead holding what looked like a potbellied mole in her manicured hands.

And one of the new babies is sick. The Kitty Angel needs a thousand dollars for special surgery or something. There's a page where you can donate.

You know, there are *people* who need that kind of money.

So?

The phone dinged in her hand, a text message bubble popping into view.

Hold on a second, Ava said.

She groaned, then began typing furiously

with her forefingers.

Oh my god, I can't believe her, she muttered. I am *so done* with Olivia — it's like she doesn't even respect the Dakota rule.

What?

When you say Dakota it means you have to keep the conversation a secret, Ava sighed, rolling her eyes as if she were explaining something simple to a much younger child. Cross your heart and hope to die. It's serious.

Ava.

And obviously Olivia knows the rule — she's known it from day one, when we first said she could hang out with us — but now she keeps going around talking about things she's not supposed to talk about.

Ava.

She's always so weird though. Yesterday during lunch everyone was trying to make Morgan feel better because her boyfriend from camp broke up with her, and since Olivia didn't know anything about it and isn't even really friends with Morgan she literally didn't know what to do, so she just took out her phone and started taking pictures of herself making funny faces. I mean, who was she even going to send them to? No one, that's who. Thank god we didn't let her be part of the sugar baby club —

Ava!

What?

Give me your phone.

Why?

That's part of our agreement.

What agreement?

You're in trouble, remember?

I thought you said you still loved me.

I do, but you're still in trouble. Give me the phone. Now.

She handed it over, pouting at the injustice. It reminded me of Beau's look of misery whenever we forced him outside in bad weather, a look that asked what he had done to deserve this torture.

I'll turn mine off too, so we're even, I said, taking out my own phone — this year's AiOn, with the facial-recognition software — and powering it down. We'll both be off the grid.

She rolled her eyes again and leaned back in her seat, turning her face away from me.

Do you want to get ice cream?

She shook her head. It's too fattening, she said.

Sweetheart.

I said I don't *want* any.

Okay, let's just drive then, all right? So you can calm down a little.

Can we go to the mall?

143

No.

But *Daddy* —

Fine. We'll go to the mall.

I started the car, and soon we were cruising down the long driveway, under the dappled shadows of the overhanging oaks, leaving the shame and frustration of the morning behind.

We went to the luxury mall named after a famous American poet, where verses about God and the Union dead were carved into imitation marble walls, stanzas about the dignity of the workingman wedged between awnings for Abercrombie and J.Crew. As we made our way through the mall's airy, palm-lined atria and gleaming corridors, Ava absentmindedly reached for my hand. It was during the school day, so there was no need to fear running into her friends.

In an expensive department store she paused purposefully by the makeup counter, hand on her cocked hip as she studied the shelves sorted by brand names: some childish and sassy, some elegant and European. Photographs advertised the wares — a woman with her eyelids painted like a toucan's plumage, a girl with the matte eggshell cheeks of a doll. There were rows of reds and pinks, nudes and darks, liquids, sticks, pots, needles, and other tiny phallic contraptions. There were cases of eye shadow in orderly colored squares like paint swatch samplers.

No makeup, I said.

Why?

You're too young.

I'm not too young, she retorted. I shave my legs.

You do?

I tried to.

She pointed to one smooth stripe running up her calf, the fur of her invisible golden hairs cleared away.

I used Mommy's razor. In the shower.

I'm still not buying you any makeup.

Well, what can I get then?

Who says you're allowed to get something?

Then why are we here?

We wandered into the celestial white light box of the AiOn store, where Ava walked as if hypnotized toward the long, chrome-legged blondwood tables on which various devices were arrayed, each phone and tablet propped on its own Lucite podium, their screens pulsing with Technicolor animations.

Following in my daughter's wake, I thought of a homework assignment she'd had once, back in third grade. She'd had to

145

write a poem in the voice of someone or something else — a princess, a whale, anything. Ava had refused all offers of assistance and shut herself in her room to write. Finally, at bedtime, she showed me the finished piece.

> The amazing new thing
> It's amazing, it does everything
> It's amazing, you will love it
> I promise
> Oh wait
> It stinks

See, she'd said triumphantly. I pretended to be you.

Now I watched her play with the phones, using their camera apps to give herself kitten ears, a halo of butterflies and flowers, a face like a Japanese schoolgirl's.

You want to know a secret? I asked.

Okay, she said, still absorbed in her altered reflection.

Guess whose campaign I might get to work on.

She looked up at me, sensing this was privileged information.

Whose?

First you have to say Dakota.

She snorted. Really, Daddy?

Rules are rules.

Okay, Dakota, she sighed. Now tell me.

I cast a meaningful glance around the store, then smiled back at my daughter, my forefinger pressed to my lips.

Oh my god! she gasped, her eyes wide and alight. Really?

Really.

That's *so cool*! Will I get a free one?

Probably not.

Oh, come on, she said, but she was grinning. What if I'm really, *really* good?

We'll see.

I bought her a new phone case, something pink and gold and glittery. She was definitely on the upswing now. A day with her father felt special, a break from routine. We didn't get to spend time together like this very often.

But as much as I treasured this stolen idyll, I knew that I still needed to talk to my daughter about what she had done. I knew I'd be failing her as a parent if I didn't try everything in my power to make her understand that she could never do anything like that again.

As we left the store, I looked down at her bare arm and noticed the two small beauty marks near her elbow had been connected

147

by a fingernail curve of blue pen — a smiley face.

I took the parkway south and drove us out to the beach, the same one we always visited. It was a windless day, the ocean the deep sapphire of the off-season, the parking lot nearly empty. Far off to our west, a lone figure in a bomber jacket was feeding seagulls. The birds crowded at his feet, a carpet of supplicants, and when he stepped toward them they threw themselves up into the air as one great mass. We got out of the car and walked toward the water, squinting against the brightness of the sand.

When she was four or five, Ava lost one of her dolls here. We were halfway home when she realized it. She threw a fit, and though it was already getting dark, I turned the car around so that we could go back and search. Ava roamed around the sparse groupings of people still left on the beach — mostly college kids drinking, or couples looking for privacy — and asked everyone if they'd seen her doll. She prattled on in a plaintive singsong, her soft face torqued by worry.

Have you seen my doll? Have you seen her? She was here. I know she was here.

Miriam stood a little off to the side, pretending to look for the doll. She knew it was a lost cause.

Have you seen my doll?

As my daughter toddled past me I reached out to pat her on her head and just missed, my palm swiping an arc over the dark tendrils of her ponytail as she slipped by. I let her tire herself out, knowing she would take the loss hard, that it would be the first time that something she loved would never come back.

Years later, I would think of that hopeless search as I watched the news one night and saw a quartet of men in Day-Glo windbreakers trekking over those same windswept dunes, the iron winter ocean roiling behind them.

They were looking for bodies.

In the end, they found around a dozen, scattered throughout the marshland near the parkway. Mostly skeletal remains in sacks, skulls and teeth buried in the sand. They uncovered a mother and blanketwrapped baby together, but the rest of the victims were young women. Prostitutes.

You've heard about these murders, these women. They advertised themselves as escorts online, posting photos of themselves smiling toughly, hiding their bad teeth.

They took the work to pay their rent, to feed their kids, to secure whatever substance they had allowed to enslave them. They wanted to escape their lives of struggle and drudgery, to run away from the degradations of the stockroom, the fast-food counter, the hotel laundry, the gas pump. They wanted money and respect, wanted to star in a more exciting movie of their own lives. To them, a thousand dollars meant the world. They told themselves they were just dancing. Just going on dates.

Poor girls, lost girls, powerless to escape their pasts, crushed by the facts of where they came from. Like Eurydice following Orpheus, they'd almost climbed out of hell, only to lose their grip at the mouth of the cave and fall farther than before. They died afraid, with sand in their mouths.

I pitied them, but they also disgusted me. I didn't understand how they could risk their lives like that when they were so close to getting away.

And though I knew on some level it was paranoid and extreme to equate what Ava had done with what these women had done to themselves, I also knew the line between the two was there, waiting to be drawn. Some of these women had come from good families with concerned parents. Who knows how many seemingly minor transgressions they'd amassed throughout their youths, their lapses collecting unnoticed like plaque in an artery, building toward a blockage? There was always a tipping point. If you weren't careful, you could succumb to its gravity without even knowing you were falling.

Near the water's edge, but still a safe distance from the surf, I put my arm around my daughter and we looked down at our conjoined shadows spilled across the sand.

Ava, I began. Sweetheart.

Yeah?

This is serious. We need to talk about what you did.

She sighed in resignation, her head listing to lean against my chest.

Why did you do it? I asked softly.

She shrugged. We thought it was funny, she said. It was just supposed to be a joke.

But you see how it's not funny, right? I said. You see how it could be dangerous?

How?

People might think you're being serious, that you're actually offering what you're advertising. They might try to come find you.

But how can they think that? We're just kids. We wouldn't actually —

Some people don't care, I said. That's what they're looking for.

151

Gross.

Do you even know what a sugar baby is?

Isn't it just, like, a sweet girl?

Oh, Ava.

She turned to look out at the sparkling blue plain of the ocean and lifted a hand to brush back her hair, the way an actress might perform a moment of quiet reflection. I watched my daughter scan the horizon, watched her observe herself being observed in her pose of contrite contemplation.

We just wanted to look pretty, she said, a tremor in her voice. We wanted to look older.

You don't need to look older, I said. You'll be older soon.

Too soon. She was in such a hurry to get there, running recklessly into her future.

I just want you to be safe, I said. That's all I want. Okay?

Okay.

I kissed her on the forehead. I considered telling her about the murdered women, as a cautionary tale. But I knew she was much too young for all that. She wouldn't understand; it would only frighten her.

A memory comes back to me. A warm afternoon in Evie's top-floor studio shortly after our father died, breeze stirring the kente cloth curtains, sounds of traffic and shouts of pedestrians wafting up from the sidewalk and through the open windows.

The apartment is small but bright. There are a few limp plants clinging to life; rocks and shells and sea glass collected at the beach are scattered along the windowsills. The careful wreck of a young woman's first home.

Evie is carrying a tray with tea things over from the corner kitchenette; she sets it down on the trunk she uses as a coffee table and sits on the floor in front of me. She is laughing, copper and silver bracelets jangling on her wrists. Her loudly patterned dress is too large for her, open at the neck, loose on her shoulders.

It's great actually, she is saying. The dates pay really well, and it doesn't even feel like work most of the time. A lot of them are actually really nice. And of course it's only for now. When we get a record deal I'll stop. Here, drink this.

We clink our chipped mugs together. I take a sip of vile, bitter tea, and Evie laughs at the face I make.

It's supposed to be good for your immune system, she says. And your energy.

Then she is handing me an envelope

labeled with my name in exclamatory all caps.

Take this, she says. Give some to Mom and the twins. I have plenty. I even have a safe deposit box now, at the bank.

Her hair is longer than it's ever been. Dark strands of it are caught in her fingernails; modest nests of it lie forgotten on the floor.

I'm writing a book too, she says. About my life. Starting when I was a kid. With Daddy and everything.

I don't say anything, even though I know she expects me to, even though she's staring at me, waiting for me to speak.

Don't do that, she says finally.

Do what?

Act as if you don't know what I'm talking about.

I just don't know what to say to you.

Well think of something.

Evie, come on.

You always acted like you didn't know what was happening. You never helped me.

She scratches at her wrists, tearing at the skin in the gaps between the armor of the bracelets. There's a rash in the bend of her arm, a thatch of jam-colored welts.

But I did help, I say. I tried to protect you.

She laughs at me.

I *did*! I insist. Don't you remember that

154

night I threw him down the stairs?

He *fell* down the stairs, Thomas. And at that point it had been going on for years. It hardly mattered anymore.

What else could I have done? I say helplessly. I was just a child.

You were, weren't you?

She turns away from me and looks around the room, her chin raised, admiring her things.

Forget it, she says lightly. I don't want to talk about it anymore. It's over.

Evie, I plead, reaching my hands toward hers. She moves them away before I can touch them, clasping them together and hiding them in her lap. She closes her eyes.

I just feel like my life is finally beginning, you know? she says, her eyes still shut tightly against me, as if willing me to disappear. After all that bullshit. Everything just feels possible now.

I don't ask her what she means. For some reason, whenever I remember this moment I hear the Queen of the Night's aria, from Mozart's *Magic Flute,* the soprano's raging coloratura runs rising from the radio like an alarm, but I know this is impossible, because Evie never listens to opera. Not since she was a child.

■ ■ ■ ■

Back in the car, Ava drowsed, cradled in her sun-warmed leather seat, as I drove us back over the bridge. I still didn't want to go home, still didn't want our day together to end. I knew we wouldn't have many days like this left. Hardly conscious of making the decision, I took the first exit off the parkway and eased through the familiar bends of Main Street, then down the long, hedge-shaded lane to the old house.

It had been a while.

The pool was covered for the season, a pit shrouded by a moon-like skin. The backyard was quiet, matted with fallen leaves, chambered by cold shadows. I stood on the patio, surveying the low boughs of dead trees dangling like dark arms over the fence. I'd have to hire someone to cut them down before it snowed.

How about a cookie?

Or a piece of cake?

My sisters' voices, drifting out through an open window. Ava was with them.

No — no thanks, she said. I'm fine.

You have to eat, baby girl. You're getting too skinny.

I'm fine.

How about a drink? Coke?

Diet Coke.

Okay, but with a scoop of ice cream in it.

No thank you.

Come on — just a spoonful.

Fine.

I went inside, hovering in the doorway between the dining room and kitchen as the twins fussed over Ava, clearing their water-colors, empty soda bottles, magazines, and half-eaten plates of food off the crowded table to set her up with her snack.

Though their heads were still crowned with the same knots of ruby and sapphire, my sisters had changed in other ways over the years. They had grown fleshy in strange places, like ill-formed sculptures — their faces were jowly, and they had the thin arms and distended bellies of starving children. In the cluttered sunroom, they painted enormous abstract canvases of naked women, close-ups of psychedelic genitalia. They could cook now — they baked cinnamon breads, simmered great vats of spaghetti and meatballs, and roasted whole ducks — and they washed everything down with wine coolers or sodas spiked with vodka and rum. I'd been relieved to find them fully clothed when we'd arrived that afternoon — they often flounced around the

157

house in states of undress, and you couldn't always count on them to throw on a robe before they came to answer the door.

When Ava was still very young, I'd sat my sisters down for a serious talk and told them if they wanted to have any kind of relationship with my daughter, they would have to be on their very best behavior and respect the boundaries that I dictated.

No sex talk, I'd said. No skinny-dipping. And absolutely no stories about Evie or Dad. Or else no Ava. Ever.

They had avoided my eyes throughout my whole speech, refusing to show any sign of recognition or assent — like a pair of chastened dogs who knew they were in trouble but didn't have the mental capacity to understand why.

What if we mess up? Kit had whispered finally. Like, on accident?

Don't.

What if we do?

Just don't.

So they tried their best to be normal, for the sake of their niece. They'd been brought up as dolls themselves, and now they had their own little doll to adore.

And despite what you might have expected based on her cool-girl public persona, Ava adored my sisters. Having a pair of extremely weird aunts conferred a certain exoticism, a flavor of fantasy, as if she were a Disney princess attended by magnanimous fairies. Ava loved the old house and the way she was treated when she came to visit: diet soda with her breakfast in bed, hours of television and movies after midnight, her favorite books piled on the canopy bed in the third-floor room that she had claimed as her own — Tolkien, Anne Rice, *Where the Red Fern Grows.*

She was basking in the glow of their ministrations now, happily sucking up the sallow foam of her ice cream float. My sisters danced around her, tidying their hoarded clutter and chattering away. They all seemed to have forgotten I was there.

So, are we playing hooky today? Kit asked. What's the occasion?

I got in trouble, Ava sighed.

You? In trouble? Deedee mock gasped. Miss Perfect? I don't believe it.

It was stupid, Ava said, looking at her hands and reddening slightly. I made a really big mistake.

Well, sweetheart, we don't have to talk about it, Kit said, pulling up a chair, motioning for Deedee to join their conference at the table. Tell us what else you've been up to.

Daddy picked me up from school and we've just been driving around. We went to the mall and I got a new phone case.

Lucky you.

And then we went to the beach.

Did you sunbathe? Or go in the water?

No, we just talked.

It's a good place for a conversation, isn't it? Deedee said, her hands working through Ava's dark hair, beginning to braid it. Your daddy learned that from us.

When we were younger we used to beg him to take us out there, just so we could get out of the house, Kit added. Every time he came to visit we'd invent some excuse for going out, and then we'd ask him drive us to the beach.

Just so you could talk? Ava asked. Why couldn't you talk at home?

My sisters exchanged glances over Ava's head, a silent transmission passing between them. I couldn't understand why they were being so conspiratorial, why they were throwing a curtain of intrigue over the mundane routines of their youth, making up a story for Ava's benefit.

It was just different, Kit said finally. It was different being out of the house.

What would you talk about? Ava asked.

Oh, I don't know, Deedee said, still looking at Kit, who sat slumped in her chair, engrossed in picking at her cuticles (she'd never managed to improve her posture, no matter how often I pointed it out, trying to help her). We'd talk about what we would do when we got older and were allowed to get a place of our own. Back then we really wanted to move out.

Why?

We'd just been home for so long. You know, for years and years. We hadn't really been in school since before we were your age.

But that sounds so fun! I wish *I* didn't have to go to school.

It was okay for a while. But when we got older it wasn't so fun.

We weren't kids anymore.

For a while they sat without speaking — Deedee focused on the careful gathering and weaving of Ava's hair, Kit focused on the diligent mangling of her own fingernails. Paused in these poses of rumination, they seemed to be putting on a performance, acting out the sense of longing and regret that suited their invented narrative of thwarted hopes.

But you ended up staying anyway, Ava prompted, breaking the silence.

Of course they had stayed. They had

161

stayed because they had never really dreamed about leaving home or doing something else with their lives. They had never wanted to.

That we did, baby girl, Deedee said, patting the finished braid against Ava's nape. That we did.

Did you stay because of Grandma?

You could say that, yes.

Something else was troubling me now. By this point in the visit I'd have expected my mother to make an appearance, shuffling into the kitchen to say hello to her granddaughter, but there was still no sign of her.

Where is Ma? I asked suddenly.

In her room, Deedee said, not looking at me. She's taking her nap.

This seemed wrong to me. Of course these days my mother slept a lot — even more than she used to — but for some reason I'd been sure that she would be awake when we came over. There had to be a reason for my certainty.

Doesn't she have physical therapy today? I asked. Shouldn't she be getting ready?

No, that's Tuesdays and Thursdays.

Are you sure? I pressed. It's always been Wednesdays and Fridays. When did it change?

It didn't change, Kit said. *We* changed it.

But why?

Why do you care? Deedee asked. You're not the one who brings her.

She had a point. They did do all the driving — after years of avoidance and crying fits when I tried to teach them, they'd both managed to pass their road tests on their third try after Ma started showing symptoms — but it wasn't fair to say they did everything.

No, I just pay for it, I said.

Ava was watching us, her eyes following our volleys, her gaze uneasy. When she caught me looking at her she stared down at the table, her mouth suddenly small in her face.

Do you want us to read your cards, baby girl? Kit asked brightly, brandishing the old battered box with the evil eye. We haven't done them since last spring.

Ava looked up and nodded, relieved.

It's good to do it at least twice a year, Deedee said. Helps keep your clarity.

I wish your mommy would let us read hers, Kit sighed, passing the deck to Ava. She hasn't wanted to in years.

Why not? Ava asked, taking the cards in her small hands, trying to rearrange them.

I walked away before I could hear my sisters' response. I didn't want to listen to any more of their made-up stories.

The faucet in the upstairs bathroom had been leaking for a long time. A rusty comet of a blemish marked the ceramic bowl of the sink, the track corroded by the inexorable drip of hard water. I thought I could probably repair the leak myself, but I knew it would be impossible to find a wrench without turning the house upside down. I'd have to come back and do it another day.

They still counted on me to fix everything in this house. The sheer scope of the upkeep could be overwhelming at times, but I tried to limit myself to small acts of restoration — things that absolutely needed to be done, or things that would be noticed and appreciated. It was a comfort to think of my mother and sisters living securely in a house that I maintained. I took care of them, and I always would.

I wandered around the rest of the upstairs, checking on what else needed to be done. Burned-out bulbs in the hallways, a broken window sash in the twins' room. I noticed they had pushed their beds together, their restless bodies imprinted in the disheveled sheets. I tried not to think about what kind of unnatural games they played in there at night.

Though parts of the mural had faded and chipped away over the years, the remains of Evie the angel still languished on the wall, looking down on me with blank eyes.

There was an unmistakable, rainy forest smell of decaying wood throughout the top floor. The walls must have been rotting, their ruin still hidden behind the brocade wallpaper. When I opened the door to the spare room I could hear scrabblings in the eaves, the sounds of some creature trying to get out.

Downstairs, her tarot reading over, Ava was swaddled in an afghan on the living room couch, her heavy-lidded eyes fixed on the television, staring at the screen with a look of ennui — my cold and jaded Princess Turandot.

It had been a long and tiring day for her. I would take her home soon.

I found my sisters at the kitchen table, both of them bowed over a magazine spread of an actress and her newborn, their cheeks nearly touching, Deedee massaging the back of Kit's neck as Kit traced lopsided circles on Deedee's knee with her forefinger. They'd been talking quietly, but they fell silent and moved away from each other when I entered the room. It felt as though they were holding their breath.

Why are you telling her this stuff? I asked.

They looked up at me, their eyes wide and guileless.

What stuff?

Why are you lying to her?

Lying?

All that stuff about you wanting to leave home.

We're not lying, Thomas.

You *never* wanted to leave home, I insisted. And you certainly never said anything to me about it. Never.

Yeah we did, Kit said. You just don't remember.

Or you don't want to remember, Deedee added.

You think I'm going to trust your version over mine? Just because you *wish* you'd done things differently doesn't mean things actually happened that way. And you have no right to blame anything on me.

Well it doesn't matter now, does it? Kit snapped. It's just water under the fucking bridge, isn't it?

I have no idea what you're talking about, I said.

Just say we're crazy, Deedee sneered. Just say it. We know that's what you're thinking. You've always thought it.

Their brains had been addled by years of

isolation and junk, their memories distorted by their disappointment. They were just like Evie, telling lie upon lie to make things sound better than they really were. Even worse, for some reason they had cast me as the villain in their fabricated drama. In their minds, I was the older brother who had refused to help, when in fact all I had ever done was provide for them and do everything in my power to give them a better life. How could they not see that?

I just give you money, that's all, I said, hurt by their ingratitude. A quarter of each paycheck, out the window. All for you.

A quarter? Deedee sighed. Please, Thomas. It barely covers what we need.

You think it's easy? I said. You think the money just magically appears in my account? I *work* for a living. That's money for my wife and daughter.

Such a martyr, Kit said. We see you're really suffering.

Yeah, is that a *twenty-fifteen* Mercedes? Deedee asked, rolling her eyes. How embarrassing for you.

Stop it.

If we didn't clean and babysit for the Cohens we probably wouldn't be able to keep the lights on.

They were being cruel now, taking out

their misery on me, strafing me with it.

I'm taking my daughter home, and I don't have to bring her back here again.

You wouldn't do that.

Watch me. I'll do whatever I have to do.

But Ava wasn't in the living room anymore. I searched the house for her, calling her name — not urgently, not anxiously, just calling for her. On the second floor I saw that the door to my mother's room was ajar, a stripe of late-afternoon sun leaking through the narrow gap, etching a path of light on the worn oriental rug. I knocked softly.

Come in, someone whispered.

Ava sat balanced on the foot of the bed, her sneakered feet dangling. My mother lay on her back, the blank mask of her face nestled in her heap of mismatched pillows, her thin and sinewy arms rigid at her sides. The medication helped with the tremors, but it couldn't hide the fact that she'd become a dry and quivering husk of herself — a mumbling, shuffling wraith, forever in danger of falling.

It's late, I said. We have to go home.

My mother's lips moved, and Ava bent to listen to her silent words.

She wants us to stay a little longer.

I nodded and sat down in the old wing-

168

back chair wedged in the corner. My mother closed her eyes, and we listened to her breathe, the sound both hard and weak. I picked up a section of the *Times* and began to page through it, my eyes skimming over last week's movie reviews.

Suddenly my mother's breathing changed, an abrupt pause in the labored in and out. She opened her eyes and looked at Ava, whispered something else I couldn't hear.

No, it's okay, Ava said. We don't mind.

My mother nodded and dozed again. I exchanged a look with Ava, sharing a sad half smile. Other children would have been frightened to be around someone so sick, but her grandmother's illness never bothered her. She was too good, too loving to be afraid.

And that was why I could never actually follow through on my empty threats to my sisters — after all that my mother had suffered, I could never keep her one and only grandchild away from her.

We sat there for a while longer, until finally I nodded to Ava and we left my mother to sleep undisturbed.

Driving home on the parkway, Ava nodding off beside me, I listened to the end of a story on NPR about growth-attenuation therapy for severely disabled children.

Unable to care for themselves, entirely dependent on their parents, these children would only become more of a burden as their bodies grew and developed. As they aged, it would become harder to hold them, harder to move them. And so these children were given doses of estrogen to close their growth plates, hysterectomies to sterilize them. Their breast buds were removed and their puberty was halted. Their parents would be left with a smaller, more manageable child — a child who would stay a child forever.

She's going to be a baby for all her life, one mother said, unrepentant. I need to be able to hold her for all of mine.

I'm just trying my best, she added.

Her voice faded into the trills of dueling marimbas, the story subsumed by an interlude of African jazz. Then the news: another stabbing at a train station in Paris, wildfires in the Pacific Northwest, late-season hurricanes pummeling the Gulf Coast, sixty-year sentences for inauguration protestors, the settlement of a lawsuit over cancer-causing weed killer.

I changed the station and was pleased and relieved to find myself wandering the haunting, atonal landscape of Alban Berg's *Lulu*

170

with the German soprano Marlis Petersen (a two-decade veteran of the title role, she was rightfully considered *the* essential Lulu — there would never again be another like her). The star-crossed, despoiled heroine had just escaped from prison; I listened as we climbed through the groves of our neighborhood, the houses growing larger with each gentle bend and hill, sun flashing through the gaps in the yellowing oaks. I glanced over at my daughter and watched for a moment as the shadows from the overhanging trees shifted over her placid face, as Lulu interrupted her lover's heart-felt serenade to ask if this was the sofa where his father had bled to death at her hand.

It wasn't until I pulled into our driveway and saw Miriam's car that I remembered our phones had been off all day.

Don't get upset, I said.

Miriam was pacing around the kitchen, her knuckles pressed to her mouth as she tried to stifle her sobs. Ava was in her room. I had wanted to talk to my wife about our daughter's digital indiscretions, but she refused to calm down and listen to me.

I had no idea where you were! she kept

crying. I couldn't reach either of you for hours!

I know, I know, I'm sorry, I sighed. I already said I was sorry. Why are you being so hysterical?

We were supposed to be there in time for dinner. And now the traffic — we'll never —

Look, just calm down, I said. I'll call Josh and Sadie and tell them something came up. We'll leave first thing in the morning. It's not a big deal! Can you just calm down?

You can't do things like this!

Things like what?

You can't just take our daughter places and not tell me! When I finally called the school and they told me you'd picked her up I just — I just —

You didn't just assume that she was safe with me?

I didn't know what to think!

I can't believe you, I said. I can't believe what you're saying.

They told me there had been an incident, that she had done something online.

Yes, we have to talk about it, I said. I have everything saved to show you. But you need to calm down first.

No, I want you to tell me now! Show me now!

We can't do anything until you calm down.

She was hunched over the sink now, bracing herself against the counter with both hands, trying to catch her breath.

I'm going to order dinner, I said. Chinese okay with you?

She didn't answer. Her back to me, she stared out the window at the fading patches of light in the backyard grass, into the dark wall of pines that shielded us from our neighbors. I could see that the psoriasis on the nape of her neck had gotten worse, raw red scales spreading like blight over the knots of her spine.

Chinese it is, I said.

After dinner and an hour of television — some continuing saga about a family of rich girls shopping and crying in Morocco — we put Ava to bed. Miriam went in first; I heard her moving around the room, putting things away, speaking to our daughter in French, which she did very rarely. She knew I didn't like being left out of the conversation like that.

Then it was my turn to enter the dimly lit periwinkle cove of Ava's room, her cozy shrine to girlhood. She was safe in there, surrounded by her pindot wallpaper, her black-and-white prints of cobblestoned Parisian alleys, her glow-in-the-dark constellation stickers, her bookshelves crowded with framed family photographs and minia-ture ceramic kittens and the small army of her soccer trophies — little golden kickers, frozen mid-stride, their ponytails like flags flying behind them. She was sitting up in her narrow bed, her small hands hidden in the folds of her white comforter, her menag-erie of stuffed animals huddled at her feet.

Is Mommy mad at me?

No, she's not mad at you.

She's upset though.

What do you mean? I asked, a catch in my voice. What did she say?

Ava ignored me for a moment, pitching forward to gather up a stuffed black lamb she had always been partial to.

I don't know, she said, hugging the lamb by its neck. She didn't really *say* anything — I can just tell she's upset.

She's fine, I said, bending to kiss my daughter's forehead. Don't worry about her.

When I came back downstairs Miriam was sitting at the kitchen island looking at my laptop screen, her face wet with tears. She didn't look up. I poured myself a few fingers of scotch and leaned against the counter, watching my wife cringe as she enlarged each image.

So, you see.

She was silent.

You see this kind of thing can't continue.

She sighed heavily, resting her chin in her hand.

Then what do we do? she asked finally.

No internet, I said. We take away her laptop and phone. She's lost those privileges.

No internet at all?

None.

But she needs it for school, Miriam said. For research.

She'll use one of our computers, and we'll monitor it.

For how long?

I shrugged.

Until we can trust her again.

I just think — I mean —

What?

I know this is bad, she said. But I wonder if there's anything else we can do. You know, talk to her about things.

Talk to her? You think this is a problem that can be solved by *talking*?

She must be acting out like this for a reason, Miriam said. Girls start going through so much when they're this age — it can be very hard for them. Don't you want to understand why she would do something like this?

No, not particularly, I said. I just want it to stop.

If all we do is punish her, the only thing she'll learn from this experience is that she can't trust us.

I don't fucking care what she learns! Don't you want her to be safe? She can't learn anything if she's been abducted by some predator who comes to collect his child prostitute!

Thomas, stop.

What?

You're being irrational.

I'm being irrational? I am? I'm surprised you don't seem to care about our daughter's safety. Our eleven-year-old daughter!

I just think we should talk to her.

I already talked to her. There's nothing else to talk about, I said. End of story.

Thomas —

I said *end of story*!

She stared at me for a long beat, panting slightly — at first I thought she was gathering her strength for another assault, but as the seconds passed I realized she was merely exhausted from her exertions. Surrendering.

Fine, she said at last. Story over.

I know this is for the best, I said. We're making the right choice.

I thought you said end of story! she jeered at me with sudden venom. Why are you writing an epilogue?

Oh, fuck off, I said, throwing up my hands.

I went out for a walk. Our neighborhood was quiet at night, not a trace of human activity in its winding avenues and ample lawns, just the fitful sounds of the breeze and the long chirps of late-season crickets. I missed the old sodium streetlights, the way they warmed your path, the way their jaundiced halos bloomed in the canopies of the trees. The new blue LED bulbs made the streets look like a film set, blasting corners with a harsh, disinfectant glare.

I walked down the middle of the road. I could see inside some of my neighbors' houses, their windows glowing in the darkness like dioramas of model homes: a teenage girl and her father washing dishes, a trio of children eating ice cream at a kitchen counter, a husband and wife side by side on a long sofa, light from a television flickering on their faces.

The events of the day weighed heavily on me. It had hurt me to see Miriam so upset; it seemed I could go nowhere and do nothing without my best intentions being ignored or misinterpreted, the women in my family chafing against my efforts to protect and provide for them.

Was I wrong? Was I being myopic, reactionary?

Miriam was also a provider. She gave us love and emotional support, and brought order to the household. Our family certainly wouldn't function without her.

Then again, the girls *couldn't survive* without me. Sure, I could be one of those parents who approached the dangers of growing up with a sense of nuance. I could do as Dr. Hanover had said and always begin by listening. I could be permissive like my sisters, wistfully romanticizing life's potential. I could allow my daughter to make and learn from her own mistakes.

But none of it would matter at all if I couldn't protect her.

As often happened in times of stress, my thoughts drifted to work. The AiOn account was important, prestigious; securing it would be an enormous accomplishment. The brand had a long and illustrious history of innovative, iconic ads; their campaigns were always models of aesthetic clarity and emotional storytelling. They'd specifically asked our agency to develop a pitch for their new smartphone campaign because they admired our other work; the creative brief generated by our account manager had emphasized that AiOn wanted a powerful, moving story about what it means to be connected in today's world.

As I walked on I began to sense the genesis of a new idea the way I usually did, visualizing moments like film clips in my mind, the vivid beginnings of a story. I saw husbands and wives, parents and children, brief but evocative scenes cohering around crucial questions and universal concerns. What does it mean to be in touch? Why do we need to be connected? Moment by moment, I could see the pitch beginning to take shape. It would be poignant and compelling, a story suited to the realities of the present. People would talk about it for years.

When I got back to the house, Miriam was waiting for me in the living room. She sat curled up in a corner of the couch, her hands folded in her lap, her feet tucked beneath her, warm light from the table lamp shining in her damp eyes and on the crown of her hair, catching the family diamond on her left ring finger.

I'm sorry, darling, she said quietly, looking into my face. You're right.

She was softer now, gentler, the way I always knew her to be. I moved toward her, folded her into my arms and kissed her, and then we didn't talk for a long while.

That night in the kitchen, after Miriam had gone to sleep, I deleted everything. First Ava's various social media accounts, then the original files for the offending images she'd uploaded to the sugar baby profile — anything that had been saved on her phone or computer.

At first I went quickly, trying not to absorb any details, but then I paused to look at the main image again, the one I had seen in Dr. Hanover's office. The pose. The parted lips. The promise to be a bad girl.

My daughter.

Acid shot up my throat, and I made it to the downstairs bathroom just in time, my right shin bashing into the toilet base as everything in my stomach was strangled out of me. Afterward, I lay curled on my side with my cheek on the cold tiles and thought of Evie — what had been done to her, what she had done to herself. What I had failed to do for her.

It was unthinkable that I could ever be so passive again — that I could ever abandon my Ava to the same fate.

When I was sure I could get up and go on without any more heaving, I returned to my labors. I came to the other photographs, the folders upon folders of my daughter's portraits. Not selfies; these were no candid, careless snapshots. Each frame had been carefully staged and art-directed, each picture taken by a discerning and trusted hand. There was Ava on the beach, her Giacometti shadow pulling her toward the placid surf. There was Ava lying on her back on a pool float wearing heart-shaped sunglasses. There was Ava grinning as she bit into a burger, her mouth highlighted in red lipstick — whose? There was Ava fingering her dark hair, gazing down in mock modesty to admire the way her pink chiffon slip dress hung from her body. They were images of a girl I'd never met, a girl I did not know. An individual, a separate person.

I began to delete these photographs as well, cursor hovering over the trash can icon as I scrolled through, each square of life evaporating into a blank at my touch. The same message popped up again and again, each new entreaty rising up faster than I could dismiss it. I clicked again and again, staring at the screen.

Are you sure you want to delete? This action cannot be undone.
Are you sure you want to delete?
Are you sure you want to?

Are you sure?
This action cannot be undone.

III

Snow is falling. I can see flakes drifting through the hazy amber beacons of the streetlights high above me, soft specks of static falling and falling through the night. The snow falls on my shoulders and hair, dusting me with white as I walk, but somehow I'm still warm and dry. The trees are bare, their feathery black branches like spiderwebs in the orange and lavender sky. Our street is empty and silent, yawningly wide.

It doesn't snow like this very often anymore. Not this time of year.

I come to what I know is our house, although it does not look like our house at all. It is larger than I remember, much taller. A tower. Through an open, lighted window I see my wife, her bare arms hanging down from the sill. She is watching me, holding her breath, keeping herself very still. The window seems impossibly high, like the

183

hatch of an oubliette.

It's the same way the window looks from my bed here, that small square of sky so far above me. Early each morning I watch the darkness drain away, waiting until I see the sharp etchings of bare branches revealing themselves, still there.

My wife is gesturing to me now, jerking her arms, trying to get my attention. Maybe she is calling out to me. She is a shadow, silhouetted by the warm light behind her. I cannot see her face, her eyes, or the movement of her mouth. She touches her throat. And now I see another figure behind her, a wraithlike woman with very long hair. Evie. They are both leaning out the window now, looking down at me, their faces close together.

Suddenly I know what will happen. I begin to call up to them. I shout at them to stay back, to get inside, to close the window. I plead with them to be careful.

This time Evie doesn't jump. She falls. She slips out the window headfirst, her hair streaming like water against the side of the house, pulling her downward. She lands some distance from me, crashing through the hedges, her body shattering into a bloody litter of rock and sea glass, shell and bone. I open my mouth but nothing comes out.

Then my wife falls, tipping forward over the sill with her hands still at her throat, as if she were gagging, as if the house had vomited her up. She lands in the soft sand at my feet, naked but not bloodied, a cuff of shadow around her broken neck.

It shouldn't be too late, I think. I should still be able to save her. I know that if I just gather her up in my arms and carry her back into the safety of the house, she'll be all right.

I could have done it. It all could have gone another way.

I look up and see my daughter standing in the window now. She is facing away from me, turned around to show me the back of her head. My heart seizes, stops. I try to scream to my daughter, but she can't hear me over the roar of the white-capped waves. I begin to run, racing over the windswept dunes toward the house, but I know it's no use. I already know she will fall.

Things move a bit faster now, I'm afraid.

December in New York City. Strings of yellow lights coat the slender trunks and gnarled branches of the elms on Sixth

Avenue. Slow caravans of tourists move through the streets like crowds of pilgrims or refugees, a never-ending crush of bodies streaming up from the bowels of Penn Station and traversing the ten blocks north to the glitchy yet regulated digital fever dream of Times Square. Steam rises from manholes, mingling with the cloying smell of roasted nuts. Profusions of green and garnet holiday coffee cups overflow the corner trash cans. The first early snowfall has melted and refrozen into a brittle skin of soot, concentrated around the curbs and corners where crowds of uncertain pedestrians dawdle and grim-faced Samaritans in shoddy Santa hats ring bells and gesture to rubber cauldrons.

It is the season for polar bears and white teeth, glitter and cashmere. Billboards show scenes from aspirational family albums: the members of a large, diverse clan pose before their stone manse, uniformed in coordinating tartan and corduroy; newlyweds in fur hats wear herringbone blazers over their holiday long johns as they romp in the snow; children in ski clothes snuggle wolfish hounds the size of horses; leggy, grinning girls link arms in sequins and taffeta, readying themselves for their midnight kisses. There is an unrelenting pressure to purchase, a pressure that masquerades as desire. It whispers, nudges: you too can own the outfit that will make you a sexy new person for the New Year; you too can find the garment that will keep you warmer than you've ever been, even though the temperature still hovers in the midforties most days.

There is an enormous Christmas tree in the lobby of my office building, a twelve-foot Douglas fir frosted with twinkling white lights and silver tinsel, weighed down by the fruit of shiny golden globes. Empty boxes wrapped to resemble gifts cower under the skirt of the low branches. An electric menorah, two of its plastic blue bulbs switched on, crouches all but forgotten on the radiator nearby.

The tree stays lit at all hours of the day and night. In the past week, I've seen it when I leave work around midnight, and again when I return before sunrise. As I come in from the darkened street, past the broad airline-counter reception desk, the empty lobby unfurls before me, its floor like the gleaming lane of a bowling alley, masonic-style marble inlays marking the path to the elevators, black lacquer and rose. I walk, my legs involuntary, barely conscious of their effort to move as I pass through the card-swipe metal detectors, around the corner into the gilded corral of the elevator bank, then into a waiting carriage to be whooshed upward with a nauseating jolt, to the thirtieth floor.

Our office spans three floors, renovated to evoke an airy luxury loft. The walls are whitewashed brick, lined with arched windows. Brass light fixtures with Edison bulbs hang over communal desks the size of dinner tables; in the corners and center of each floor are seating areas furnished with black leather Eames chairs and Scandinavian wraparound sofas. Gainsboro gray carpet muffles the murmur of voices and the syncopated birdsong of ringing telephones.

I have my own office along the western flank of the second floor, my own window that looks across the avenue to a neighboring tower, that gridded tapestry of brick and glass that walls me in. On my weathered oak French panel desk there is a curated arrangement of framed family photographs: the newlyweds on the steps of city hall, five-year-old Ava backstage at a ballet recital, the girls grinning over roadside lobsters out east last summer. The three of us on the beach in our brilliant white shirts, our faces rapturous and smug.

On the walls hang some choice pieces of Ava's juvenilia — a watercolor seascape, a

Picasso-inspired cubist self-portrait, a primitive *I LovE DAdy* illustrated by two stick figures, one big and one small, their asterisk hands joined in companionship.

I always brought Ava in for Take Your Daughter to Work Day, parking her in a corner with poster board, markers, and prints of old ads for her to collage, instructing her to design a campaign for me. At the end of the day, she'd give me her pitch.

My office, normally very neat, is a mess. My desk is crowded with papers and unwashed coffee mugs liberated from the kitchenette. A few days' worth of clothing hangs from the coat hooks on the back of the door, and takeout boxes that haven't made their way into the garbage are stacked beside the leather couch, where I've slept three of the past five nights.

But I'm not in my office right now. I'm one floor below, in the men's room. The tap of my razor against the sink bowl echoes through the silent tiled corridor of stalls. I gaze at my lathered reflection in the long mirror, pulling the blade over my skin with steady strokes, carefully controlling the slight tremor in my right hand.

I always loved being in pitch mode, pushing myself through those final frenzied days before the big presentation. It made me feel

189

incredibly powerful to prevail over the base needs of my body in order to meet my deadline and deliver a feat of creative brilliance. I was high on the familiar thrill of sleep deprivation, bolstered by the teeth-clenching rush of coffee and Ritalin and the exquisite frisson of expectation, knowing that today was the day.

After I shaved, I rode the elevator down to the temporarily vacant twenty-third floor and jogged through the abandoned space, making shark circles around the empty cubicles as the strengthening morning sun began to seep through the windows. I sang to myself, first under my breath, then louder, belting out the merry men's Anvil Chorus from Verdi's *Il Trovatore* at the top of my lungs. *So, to work now! Lift up your hammers!* On my third lap I punched a laminate partition, exultant.

Then I went back upstairs, where Carly and Abigail, the exhausted co-queens of my creative team, sat nylon knee to nylon knee on the couch in my office, awaiting my instructions.

Carly Bloom, née Moskowitz, was my art director, her third-trimester baby bump an absurd bubble on her childlike body. She'd been adopted from South Korea as an infant by the Moskowitz family of Tenafly,

New Jersey, was a graduate of RISD and CalArts. When I'd first met Carly and took in her petite frame and smart-girl glasses, I thought she looked like a pornographer's idea of an artsy working girl — shy and pretty, just waiting to take off her professional disguise. We worked very well together, Carly and I. She was clever, talented, and excellent at taking direction.

And Abigail, oh Abigail. My copywriter. She'd escaped from Baton Rouge, leaving the rest of the Landry family to their refinery jobs in Cancer Alley while she attended NYU, nursing her literary aspirations and sleeping first with her teaching assistants, then her professors. She'd told me all this one Thursday evening happy hour, her damp hand clamped on my knee as she licked her lips in a way that someone once must have told her was sexy. Abigail had published a few short stories in literary journals I'd never heard of, had been "almost done" with her first novel for the past two years. She was bottle blond, chubby, desperate to please and impress, the kind of woman who cuts her date's hair in her kitchen, famished for their love.

Good morning, ladies, I said in singsong, shrugging myself into the suit jacket I'd hung on the back of my chair. Are we ready?

They nodded wordlessly, their eyes ringed with shadows.

Game faces, my dears, I said. Let's go.

Back in October, when I'd first presented them with my concept, they had been skeptical, listening with their mouths set into unsmiling slots as I expounded excitedly on my vision for the pitch, their own mediocre, rejected ideas spread before us on the conference room table.

I don't know, Thomas, Carly said.

It sounds very . . . dark, Abigail added, careful to choose what she thought was the right word.

Definitely too dark, Carly agreed. Much too dark for AiOn.

No, I said, pacing. It's not too dark. It's a powerful vision for and about the present moment. It shows what being connected now really looks like.

But their last campaign was that history of home movies thing with all the pregnant women and dogs, Carly protested. There were babies *and* puppies in it, for fuck's sake.

Exactly, I said. Their *last* campaign. They're coming to us for something different. Something memorable, something with social impact.

It just seems grim, Abigail said. I mean, personally I'm intrigued — I *like* dark — but I'm not sure people want to be reminded of this shit when they're thinking about which smartphone to buy.

I mean, it *does* do a good job of capturing the zeitgeist, Carly allowed, her small hand resting on the rise of her belly. But I don't know if the clients will like it.

Listen, I said, bracing myself against the conference table, leaning over to look into each of their faces. If you two want to make names for yourselves and get ahead in this industry you have to be willing to take risks and be bold. Otherwise there's no point in even showing up. The world has become more radicalized, and we need to keep up and be more radical ourselves. To be honest, I expected much more from you both. I know you're capable of doing brilliant things. I know you can be leaders.

I paused, letting my words sink in. I could tell from the way she tilted her head and lowered her gaze that Abigail was considering it, allowing herself to be convinced. Carly sighed and began to doodle on a piece of scrap paper, the first sign of her eventual surrender.

Trust me, I told them. It's going to be great. *You're* going to be great.

In the end, they gave me what I wanted. They always did. And I knew I could rely on them to manage the rest of their subordinates and get things in order with production and the account managers, making sure everyone fell in line.

Overall, we made a great team. Carly and Abigail worked together much more harmoniously than I had with Brian, who'd been my copywriter before I got promoted to associate creative director. Our partnership had been like a volatile but passionate marriage, our habitual disagreements and long bouts of unresolved tension punctuated by flashes of genius. We'd done some great work together, but ultimately it had been a difficult relationship, impossible to sustain over the long term. Brian was incredibly gifted, but much too sensitive — a tantrum thrower, too quick to perceive criticism where there was none, incapable of rolling with the punches. He was always acting as though he had something to prove, forever burdened by the oversize chip on his shoulder.

Things had gotten particularly strained in the last year of our partnership. The tipping point may have been the Citadella cybersecurity print ad. We'd been working late all week, brainstorming for our Friday morning meeting with the associate creative director in charge of the account. The night before, we were still in the weeds, uninspired and dissatisfied. In a conference room, over a cold, half-eaten pizza, Brian and I tried to hash it out, and after hours of dead ends, I finally thought I had something.

I got it, I said. How about this? We put a cute little girl on some shady-looking block, have her standing in front of an abandoned house, or a boarded-up storefront. You know, make it look like Detroit or New Orleans, somewhere like that.

As I spoke I began to sketch out the scene, my pen strokes cohering into the outlines of decrepit buildings, the figure of a small child. Brian watched wordlessly, his head down, his arms folded across his chest.

So she's out in this scary neighborhood, but she's surrounded by this magic bubble, I went on, beginning to draw an orb around the girl. She's safe. The copy can be something about how with Citadella, you're always safe.

Brian stared at the drawing for a long moment. He seemed even more pensive than usual, as if he were making up his mind about more than just what was in front of him.

What do you think? I asked, prodding

him. Finally he looked up, looked me in the eye.

No, he said.

No? I repeated, incredulous. Why not?

I'm not doing that, he said slowly. It's racist.

How is it racist?

It implies poverty is dangerous, he replied, a nasty, impatient edge creeping into his voice. That poor people are dangerous. And that's an extremely racist idea.

We can make the girl black, I said. Or Latina, or whatever.

That doesn't matter, Brian snapped. It's still racist.

It's not racist! I said. It's just telling a story. A good one, I might add. This is the best idea we've had so far, and I think we need to go forward with it.

You do it then, he said, standing up abruptly and putting on his coat. You write it. I won't be a part of this.

You can't leave.

And yet here I am, walking out the door.

He left. At that point, I felt I had no choice but to move forward, writing the copy myself. I stayed late, mocking everything up.

The next morning, everyone loved the concept: *Citadella: Safe Wherever You Are.* I

196

tried to share the credit with Brian, but he was silent and sullen, stalking out of the room as soon as the meeting was over.

Brian left the agency shortly after I got promoted, moving to a firm in San Francisco so he could be closer to his extended family in the East Bay. I heard he was doing well out there, that he'd been part of the team responsible for last year's award-winning Olympics ad campaign, the saccharine one with the veterans and the voice-overs by their children.

Aside from his hypersensitivity, Brian had just never managed to develop a close relationship with Greg, our agency's senior creative director, and that failure to connect had left him out in the cold.

Greg Conroy was a Jackson Heights native, Yale School of Art dropout, and ex-hippie; an ivory-maned colossus who wore Nikes with his custom suits; a year-round surfer and New York City Ballet patron with houses in Great Neck and Montauk and a pied-à-terre on East Seventy-second Street. He was a powerful man who employed the digital shorthand of a teenager in his communications, typing *u too thnx* whenever I told him to have a good weekend.

He was the only person who was allowed to call me Tom. I hadn't bothered to correct him when we first met, and now it was much too late.

Greg had reigned over our agency for the past two decades and was a huge name in the industry; he'd recognized my talents and ambition from the beginning, taking me under his wing as his protégé and encouraging me to develop my personal style while I was still an art director. He knew I'd deliver something stellar for the AiOn pitch. When I gave him the basic concept last month, paying him a visit in his expansive corner office on the floor above mine, he was thrilled with my ideas.

I'm seeing it as a socially conscious story about connection in a time of uncertainty, I said. Moments of people being drawn together, showing you how the AiOn brand can make you feel secure in today's world. Ultimately I think it will be very uplifting.

Greg nodded, looking up at me from his television-sized flat-screen monitor, pushing his glasses up the bridge of his nose with his forefinger, the glare on his lenses masking his eyes.

Yeah, absolutely, he said. The way you're describing it sounds terrific. I'm picturing an old-school Ridley Scott ad, except made like one of those interrelated story movies. You know, like the one about racism, with the car crash.

Exactly, I said. That's exactly how I see it too.

Only not too dark, Greg said. We don't want to scare them.

Of course not.

He sighed and leaned back in his leather desk chair, meaty hands laced behind his head, rotating slowly to face the skyline.

Honestly, Tom, it would be a huge relief for me if you could take the lead on this one, he said. I've got a lot on my plate right now with the Air China and Lenovo accounts — I'm back in Beijing next week, and probably again next month. Not to mention Emily's matrimonial extravaganza. It's gotten so crazy I can't even call it a wedding anymore. Circus would be more accurate. Jesus!

He closed his eyes, as if wincing in pain.

Twenty-five years old and she's got a guest list of two hundred and fifty people. Two hundred and fifty! She hasn't lived long enough to know that many people.

And of course she had to marry an actor. Actor slash producer, I mean. Excuse me. Nice kid, great kid, loves Em to death, just adores her, but who do you think will be footing the bill for the rest of their lives? Not him, certainly. We've got a hell of a prenup ironed out for them, I can tell you that.

He sat forward and assumed a sermonic position, a finger gun pointed at me in emphasis.

When your daughter grows up, offer her cash if she'll elope, he said. Ten thousand, twenty thousand, whatever. Any amount would be worth it. Trust me.

He leaned back in his chair again and spread his arms wide, opening his massive chest to me.

Look upon me! he boomed. I may appear to be a devoted father and successful businessman, but really I'm just an ATM.

We laughed at that. I always laughed at Greg's jokes — it was something I'd learned to do early on, and the strategy had always served me well.

Go forth and prosper, he said finally, waving me out.

Greg trusted me without reservation. That was the kind of relationship we had. And so I had gone forth, seeking to prosper. With my guidance, Abigail had developed a terrific script, and Carly had sketched out each scene of the commercial just as I'd imagined. We'd mocked up some beautiful storyboards to display, but the crown jewel of the presentation would be the sample video we'd commissioned. The video was a rare step for us, especially when we hadn't actually secured the account yet, but we'd hired some poor freelancer who didn't know the worth of his labor to shoot and edit it for almost nothing — amazing what you can accomplish with basic equipment and software these days. I knew it would really show AiOn what we could do.

The work had been relentless, all-consuming. And even though I loved the high-stakes excitement of pitch mode, I had to admit that there had been too many late nights these past few weeks. It was hard on the girls — my girls at home, I mean. They missed me.

At least I could look forward to their loving reception when I did come home — my daughter bounding down the stairs in her pajamas with a joyful shout, my wife greeting me with a kiss and a warm meal. Those moments did a lot to ease the strain and stress of all my hours at the office.

But one night I'd come home exhausted to find a cold and sterile kitchen, the house drained of its coziness. Ava was already in bed, and my wife sat sulking in front of the television, unfolded laundry sorted into little piles all around her. I spoke to her from the doorway.

Is there dinner for me?

She looked up from the crimson polo in her hands to regard me blankly.

There's leftover ravioli from last night.

I brought that in with me for lunch.

Oh.

She looked at her lap, then back at the television. On a drab street corner, two detectives were talking to a heavily made-up young girl in a grizzled leopard-print coat. The girl seemed to be mocking the detectives, her red mouth puckered impertinently, gesturing with a cigarette balanced between her fingertips.

Well, I think there's a shepherd's pie in the freezer, she said, still staring at the screen. Do you want me to heat it up for you?

What's wrong?

She looked up at me, startled. I'd spoken very suddenly, maybe more vehemently than I'd meant to. I was tired.

What do you mean?

You've been home all day, I said. Why haven't you done anything?

I did laundry.

Are you depressed? Is that it?

She was quiet for a moment, looking at her lap again, still gripping that polo shirt. At this rate she would need to iron it before

Ava could wear it to school.

No, she said finally.

Then I don't understand.

The girl on the screen was crying now, her mascara staining her cheeks with black crow's feet. The detectives must have said something to upset her.

Look, I sighed. I work very hard for us. I make sacrifices and put in a lot of long hours to make sure we have what we need. And I'm not saying that to make you feel guilty — it's just what I do, because I want us to be happy. But when I do come home, I expect to be treated a certain way. It shouldn't be that hard for you.

Then she laughed, my wife. She laughed in my face, an ugly bark of a laugh.

What? I demanded. What's so funny?

Did you really just say that?

What do you mean? That I want us to be happy?

No, that you expect to be treated a certain way. Mr. Big Shot, she taunted. Just listen to yourself.

I moved toward her then — I don't know why — and she threw the polo at me, hurled it, hitting me hard in the throat.

I may have thrown it back at her, I don't remember. We were both upset.

I microwaved the shepherd's pie and ate it

at the kitchen counter. When I went up to bed my wife was already asleep, her body turned away from me, her face to the wall. Though I wanted very badly to take her in my arms, I decided not to bother trying to touch her. I knew she was in the kind of state that would make her reject all my attempts at reconciliation, no matter how sincere.

Recently I'd read that in order to maintain marital harmony and satisfaction, you needed to treat your relationship like a bank account. Positive interactions — stimulating conversation, togetherness, sex, and romance — were like deposits, and negative interactions were like withdrawals. According to this theory, it was pointless to try to resolve conflicts that could never be resolved, or attempt to avoid problems that couldn't be avoided. You just needed to maintain a buffer of positivity, a healthy balance to make up for the inevitable disappointments. Research showed couples didn't even need to bother with therapy — as long as they could keep their marital bank accounts flush, they'd be happy.

I knew things would get better once I wrapped up this pitch and could get back to building that balance of positivity. I would come home in time for dinner more often. I would help around the house whenever I was asked. I'd be there for opening night of Ava's school play, even though I would have to miss the celebratory drinks after the AiOn presentation.

It had been a stressful season for everyone, really — a very bad few months around the world. They'd discovered more mass graves outside Damascus, traffic police in Tampa had shot an unarmed man while his young daughters watched from the backseat, and on a brilliantly sunny day in November three college students had set themselves on fire in front of the Capitol, burning to death to protest their imminent deportations. Scary times, everyone said. It felt as if we were all crawling toward the holidays, crushed under the weight of current events, reaching out helplessly for the comfort of our loved ones.

But now it was finally upon me: all my hard labor on the cusp of fruition, Christmas right around the corner. The night before the big day, after we'd rehearsed the presentation one last time, I broke out a bottle of pink Veuve Clicquot to reward the girls for their efforts (Abigail and I drank most of it, of course). And after Carly left, cabbing it home to her husband, dog, and duplex on the Upper West Side, Abigail and

I moved on to the Laphroaig I kept in my desk.

By that point it was late, too late for me to go home. I must have fallen asleep on my leather couch, because sometime in the night Abigail stumbled into my office and draped her body over mine, her chin on my knees and her hand splayed spiderlike on my fly, which she was struggling to free me from.

I'll call you a car, I said.

Abigail shook her head slowly, extravagantly, turning it this way and that so that it lolled against her bare shoulders. She'd taken off her sweater, was down to a chemise, navy charmeuse against her pale skin.

I don't want a car, she drawled. I want you.

Abigail, you're drunk.

Don't care. So are you.

She slithered toward my face, rutting her hips against mine, too heavy and awkward to be sinuous. Then she slumped against me with a heavy sigh. She mumbled something into my chest, but I couldn't make out her exact words.

I thought about it for a minute. I really did. It had been such a hard few weeks, and Abigail was so sweet, so pliant. A tease. I let her lie on top of me for a while longer, ran

206

my hands up and down her bare arms. I may have stroked her hair, may have applied a gentle pressure with my palm to the back of her head as her body wriggled back down mine and she finally succeeded in undoing the button of my slacks.

But I couldn't go through with it. I was a faithful person, and I'd always been faithful to my wife. I could never betray her like this. After a few more minutes of adolescent tussling I sat up.

Stop. Just stop.

She was lying still now, all the delight gone out of her. In the end I had to push her off of me.

I ordered her a car. When she was finally gone, whisked away to her Red Hook walk-up, I finished the Laphroaig and lay down to rest, trying to put the whole undignified encounter out of my mind.

But I couldn't sleep. I was too keyed up, my body clenched by a mysterious dread. It wasn't like me to feel this anxious before a presentation. Something else had to be bothering me.

I turned on the radio, and the tender chords of Schubert's Ständchen D. 957 no. 4 for Baritone and Piano filled the room. I sat down at my desk, and before I was fully conscious of what I was doing, I'd started to make a list, setting down words and numbers in a teetering column.

Mortgage — 4000
Property Tax — 1625
Tuition — 3000
Utilities — 200
PT and Meds — 450
Sump pump — 670
Landscaping — 350
Phone — 225
Internet/cable — 150
Car Insurance — 500
Ma and the Twins — 2500
Visa — 9000 balance
Amex — 4000 balance

Those were the major expenses for this month, not including food and things like that. It made me slightly sick to look at the numbers all together. The credit cards were the most worrisome — I had to pay those off as soon as possible. And I'd have to buy presents, which would set me back at least another thousand. Ava had a long list of must-have gadgets and expensive junk she thought she needed, and I'd have to get Miri a piece of jewelry, something especially nice to make up for the tension of the past few months.

We'd spend Christmas with my family, gathering in the warm chaos of the living room, a fat tree towering over us, firelight hot on our faces. The twins would attempt an overly ambitious dinner and cover the counters with plates of cookies; my mother would confine herself to an armchair and cry silently when Frank Sinatra's rendition of "O Holy Night" came on the stereo. She insisted on listening to that album, even though it made her upset. I tried to hide the CD every year but she always found it, somehow.

When we were children, Evie and I would perform homemade Christmas pageants. She would dress us in bedsheets and foil crowns and tie tinsel around our necks and wrists; one year, she fashioned a pair of angel wings for herself out of cardboard and the innards of an eviscerated feather pillow. We would prance around in front of the fireplace, singing songs and delivering dialogue of Evie's own invention — sometimes following a story, sometimes not. Our mother would watch our antics with tears glimmering in her eyes. Our father, drunk, would fall asleep.

We always went to that house for the holidays. Though Miriam and I had talked about it for years, I couldn't manage to put anything aside for us to buy our own vacation home, somewhere in the country. The best we could do was a rental for a week or two in the summer.

My salary was $150,000 a year. I had around seven thousand in checking, thirty thousand in savings, five thousand in Ava's trust that couldn't be touched, a bit over fifty thousand in my 401(k) (I'd drained it a few too many times in the past few years). Not as much of a cushion as I would have liked, and not nearly enough so that Ava would never have to worry (which was my ultimate goal), but life was expensive, and I always made it work somehow. I would get my Christmas bonus next week, and I was due for a raise in January, which would help ease the slide into the New Year. Then I'd get everything under control.

The Schubert was hopeful and mournful all at once, the deep-voiced baritone begging for a lover who would never arrive, resigned to his fate even as he pleads for her. I bent my head and let the music pass through me, breathed as if I were chanting the words myself.

Do you hear the nightingales beating?
Oh! they implore you,
With the sounds of sweet laments

Plead for me.

It was fine. It would all be fine.

They always set out a beautiful spread on pitch days — steel platters of mini bagels with pink handkerchiefs of lox, golden croissants, and Technicolor cubes of freshly cut fruit — but I didn't touch a thing. The screen and projector were ready to go, all the connections triple-checked. I paced the sunstruck conference room as Abigail and Carly sat quietly in one corner, going over their notes one last time. Earlier in the morning I'd watched Abigail for signals of distress or clinginess, but she'd apparently decided to pretend nothing had happened between us. She was a good girl, more sensible than I'd imagined. We could both just forget about the whole thing.

I gazed down into the deep, half-shadowed cavern of the street, thirty-two stories below. Tiny cars floated in silent procession through the darkness, heading north; they paused at the corner, hesitating in the intersection's triangle of light before turning out of view.

The glass door swung open, and we all stood at attention. In strode Greg, followed by a dark-suited quartet of AiOn executives, and the room filled with the murmur of greetings and introductions, pleasantries and handshakes exchanged in the usual choreography.

The executives took their seats. I studied their faces, the details of their posture and dress, but they were already familiar to me. There was Nina Boyd, AiOn's VP of marketing and communications, and a select team of her managers: Elias Shapiro, Michael Ricci, and Lakshmi Kumar. I always conducted background research on my clients, mining their social media presence to find out their hometowns, alma maters, and favorite sports teams so that I could connect with them on a more personal level. Nina had played Division I rugby at Wesleyan and was a big Democratic donor; Elias spent his summers on Fire Island and was a die-hard Mets fan. Michael kept in close contact with his family on the Ligurian coast, and Lakshmi had just renovated a brownstone in Carroll Gardens, where she lived with her partner and two-year-old daughter. This kind of information would come in handy as I built rapport. I was great at pitching, always charming and sharp. I knew exactly what to say to make people laugh, how to generate chemistry, how to win the clients' trust and affection.

Small talk slowly petered out. Greg signaled me with a nod, and I strode to the head of the conference table, my face arranged in a genial grin. After making eye contact with each executive in turn, I let my gaze settle in the empty space just above their foreheads and took a breath.

What does it mean to be connected?

I allowed the question to hang in the air for a moment, inviting my audience to engage, stirring their emotions.

Being connected can mean many things. It means talking to family on the other side of the world, sharing baby photos over thousands of miles. It means being able to access the score of the baseball game, the weather report, or the latest political news. It means always being able to reach your child, your parent, or your spouse. And it means they can reach you too.

I paused, letting my words take hold as I gathered myself.

People around the world connect with AiOn, I said. They trust AiOn. The brand is already universally recognized for its design, quality, and reliability. But how can we go further? How can we capitalize on that sense of familiarity to project a socially conscious message and show what it means to live and be connected now?

I could tell by the way they sat forward in their seats that they were eating it up, hanging on every word. Even Greg's normally enigmatic poker face seemed buoyant.

In today's world, connection is more important than ever, I went on. In the face of division, it binds us more tightly. In the face of danger, it makes us feel safe. We want to show what AiOn can do to help ordinary people like you and me navigate these times of uncertainty.

I waited a beat and made eye contact with everyone once more, going around the room and holding each person's expectant gaze, reeling them in.

Because you don't just make phones, I said finally. You make talismans for today.

I took out the projector remote and nodded to Abigail. The room went dark, and I pressed play.

The ad begins with a blurry constellation of rainbow lights. Music swells, guitars and drums and vaguely choral vocals. Focus on a pretty girl dancing at a concert, ecstatic bodies bouncing around her. Next we see two teenagers walking along a windswept pier under a heavy gray sky, their heads lowered as white waves surge around them. Then we're moving through a collage of painted signs and mouths opened in shouts, a boy with a megaphone leading a march on a bright wintry day. Each scene evokes the intimate immediacy of found footage, a distinctly human hand behind each frame, gorgeous yet somehow ominous as we cut from one story to the next and back again.

Then comes the turn, the sudden explosion into chaos.

The dancing girl ducks as the pucker of gunfire echoes through the crowd. The teens run for shelter as the hurricane bears down, fighting their way through the squall. The march dissolves into a maelstrom of fists and truncheons, a battle breaking out on the street. For a moment our young heroes are lost in the turmoil, swallowed by the storm of events.

But then, when we've almost lost hope, we find them. The dancing girl sits on a curb, wrapped in the crinkled silver cape of a disaster blanket. The teens are safe in their house, huddled together around a lantern. The boy from the march is walking away from the scrum, trying to catch his breath as he retreats down the block. We see the unmistakable tablet of the AiOn smartphone appear like a magic amulet in each of their hands.

Elsewhere, anxious parents grip their own phones, watching the news unfold in high definition on their crystal screens. They are suspended in desperation, their hearts in their throats.

Then, one by one, the calls begin to come through, the faces of their missing loved ones suddenly filling each screen. We see each of our heroes once more, their AiOns pressed to their cheeks.

> Mom?
> Mom?
> Dad?

Cut to black, and a clear voice rings out in the sudden silence:

> I'm okay.

The AiOn logo appears, that familiar stylized infinity sign like a beacon in the night. No slogan necessary.

The lights came up. Everyone blinked in the sudden brightness, squinting like newborn animals. I nodded to Abigail and Carly, and they handed out our handsome, high-gloss storyboards.

As you can see, it's a very moving story that will resonate with a broad range of consumers, I said, making a slow circuit around the room. It's socially conscious and politically engaged, but it feels refreshingly cinematic. There's tremendous digital potential for a variety of platforms, and we can even make different versions of the spot to suit different markets. It's the kind of ad that's made to go viral.

Suddenly I realized something was very wrong. The AiOn executives were barely looking at the boards, passing them down the table with little more than a cursory glance. I stopped in the middle of a sentence.

I'm sorry, I said. I meant to ask if anyone has any questions.

Their smiles had curdled into winces. Nina Boyd looked to Elias, something unspoken yet obvious passing between them. He cleared his throat and sat forward in his chair.

It's a very powerful vision, he said. But I'm afraid it may be too dark for AiOn.

We love to tell compelling stories with our advertisements, but generally we're known for nostalgia and uplift, Nina added. Those qualities have always been an essential part of AiOn branding strategy.

The others joined in, finishing each other's thoughts in mindless, lockstep chorus.

It's clear that this concept is in tune with current events —

But we wouldn't want to appear exploitative.

Or give the impression that we're using fear to sell our product.

Look, I said. I get it. It's a bold, new idea. I know it's dark. I know it's risky. But this is what the moment calls for. We live in dark, risky times. Shouldn't we acknowledge the reality people are facing today? If we want to stand out, we need to be as radical as reality itself.

Lakshmi was frowning, her face torqued by skepticism.

Didn't Lenin say that?

Say what?

That we need to be as radical as reality.

Maybe he did, I answered curtly. I don't know.

There was a strained silence.

I'm not sure if that's a message that will resonate with our board, Nina said finally. Communist revolutionary theory tends to be a hard sell in the corporate world.

Awkward laughter shuddered through the room. I felt my face grow hot. Everything was spinning out of control, spiraling into a humiliating tempest that I was powerless to stop, all because of these rubes, these cowards. Greg was trying to get my attention, but I wouldn't look at him. I could handle this.

Are you just going to play it safe and do what corporate wants? Is that what the AiOn brand is really about? Falling in line? Horrible things are happening in the world every day because too many people are just following orders and trying to play it safe. Is that the message AiOn wants to send? That life is just puppies and babies? That it's okay to be a coward and sleepwalk through the world, and that everything will be okay as long as you can play with your little gadget?

Greg sighed and shook his head. Abigail and Carly hugged the wall, shrinking into themselves. The executives just stared. No one spoke, but they didn't need to. Their faces told me everything I needed to know.

I think you'll look back on this as a mistake, I said. I think you'll wish you'd been brave enough to go through with this.

Someone sucked in a breath. I didn't bother to see who it was.

The executives left as quickly as they could, Greg following in their wake as they hustled out of the conference room. I turned to the girls, who still stood staring at me, open-mouthed and ashen.

What? I snapped. What is it?

Carly sighed and rolled her eyes, then

began to pack up her things. But Abigail held her ground, regarding me with her arms crossed over her soft breasts, the hint of a snarl playing at her lips.

What?

We *told* you it was too dark.

Oh, fuck off.

I found Greg in his office. He looked up sharply as I came in, his face dark with displeasure.

What the fuck was that? he hissed.

That was exactly the pitch I proposed to you! I protested. You said it sounded terrific.

Fuck the goddamn pitch, Tom! What were you thinking going on that fucking rant like that?

They needed to be convinced.

And you were going to do that how? By calling them cowards? Insulting their product? Quoting fucking *Lenin*?

I was just being passionate. You've always told me I need to fight for my ideas.

But I've also told you that you need to know when to let things go! You looked like a fool, and you made *me* look like a fool.

It was a great ad! I said. They were just too chickenshit to see it.

Greg shook his head, exasperated.

I should have been more involved, he muttered, as if speaking to himself. This was too important to leave to chance.

You didn't leave it to chance, I said. You left it to me. You knew you could trust me.

And clearly that was a mistake.

His anger had made him irrational, histrionic. He wasn't himself.

You don't mean that, I said. You can't —

We'll talk on Monday, Greg said coldly, turning away from me to look out at his view, to attend to his corner of the sky, his sweep of the teeming city below.

But Greg —

Just go.

I can't remember leaving the office that evening, or many details of the drive home. I vaguely recall the sudden dusk, the usual stop-and-go gridlock in Midtown, the crowds of bristling, bundled pedestrians waiting and then flowing through the crosswalks. I remember the long tube of the tunnel, the array of billboards looming over me on the other side of the river, the green go at the tollbooth. The slow procession of lights on the expressway, a broken stripe of white heading west and a broken stripe of red heading east, vessels streaking through the darkness of the island.

And I remember listening to a special seg-

221

ment on the radio: a series of different recordings of *E Lucevan le Stelle (And the Stars Shone)*, the heart-stopping aria from the final act of Puccini's *Tosca,* each clear-toned tenor offering his own interpretation of the condemned political prisoner Cavaradossi's wrenching farewell to his life and love. Soon, I began to see the aria's repetition as a perverse reprieve from the firing squad, a never-ending prelude to execution. The last sobs were drained from our hero again and again, when he already had nothing left to give:

I die in desperation, and never was life so dear to me!

The year before, I'd taken Ava to the new production of *Tosca* at the Met. I'd been eager to see the company's return to form after the ghastly Luc Bondy version's austere sets and gratuitous fellatio. Miriam had fretted that all the torture and murder might be a bit too intense for Ava, but I knew she was mature enough to handle a work of art. It couldn't be any worse than what she saw on TV.

And yet, in the final moments of the opera — when Cavaradossi lay lifeless and his lover Tosca threw herself from the parapet, when the curtain came down and the audience erupted in a thundering ovation — my daughter had looked up at me as if I'd hit her, her eyes bright with angry tears, demanding I answer for what she'd just seen.

Why are they all *clapping*? Everyone *died*!

After that, I knew that *Rigoletto* would be out of the question. If she couldn't handle the execution of political prisoners, there was no way she'd be able to stomach the tragic twist of Verdi's dark masterpiece — a father losing his only daughter to assassins he himself had hired to avenge them both.

Then again, these recollections are probably borrowed from other evenings, other drives home. I can't be sure which memories really belong to that day, which memories I've invented and massaged to fill in the gaps.

Somehow, I made it to the Hutch campus. The visitors' lot was already full, and parked cars lined the winding drive, a long row of shiny carapaces gleaming coldly in the night. Stragglers ran giddily over the snow-covered ball fields, the air thickening with their white breath as they hurried toward the neoclassical villa of the theater building. I hurried too, shivering.

By the time I climbed the theater's broad marble steps and pushed my way through its castle-gate double doors, the auditorium was dark, dense with murmurs, the play

223

about to begin. It would be impossible to find my wife, impossible to sit beside her. I settled myself into a creaking seat in the back row, still wearing my coat.

The crowd applauded in a brief, rising shriek, and then the curtain parted to reveal a cold and cheerless office, a window with a wintry city view painted into the backdrop. Faint strains of Christmas music could be heard, coming from somewhere off-stage. A homely and bespectacled girl hunched over a writing desk, her long hair shellacked with steel, her thin face set in a scowl.

Why couldn't *I* have been Scrooge? Ava had sobbed after the casting list went up. Olivia's not even *Jewish*!

Scrooge isn't Jewish either, I'd said.

But our teacher said he might be!

Really?

She said it depends on your interpretation.

Well, you're only half Jewish, I said. And you're too pretty to be Scrooge.

Now the greedy moneylender faced down her clerk, an anxious wisp of a child armored in artfully threadbare tweed, small hands in fingerless gloves.

You'll want all day tomorrow, I suppose?

If it's quite convenient, sir.

It's not convenient, and it's not fair.

But Christmas is only once a year!

Sitting there, I felt sick all over again, feverish with anger and shame. I started at the sudden commotion onstage, a hidden door in the darkness bursting open to reveal a pudgy, wild-haired girl in a tattered waistcoat, her skin and clothes pale with chalk. She lunged around the stage, dragging her boa of aluminum foil chains, wailing inconsolably.

I am here tonight to warn you, that you have yet a chance and hope! A chance and hope to escape my fate!

The ghost began to chase after Scrooge, the two barely holding back giggles as they capered madly around the room, until finally the miser leapt into bed and burrowed under the covers, howling, a bit too gleefully, for mercy.

I thought of my wife, my dear and gentle wife. My sweet Miri. I recoiled at the thought of everything she'd had to suffer these past few weeks — everything *we'd* had to suffer — and all for nothing. I hadn't even texted her to tell her about the failure of the presentation. It was much too shameful to admit defeat after all I'd been through, after how hard I'd tried.

I had to do better. I had to try harder.

I thought of all the things I could say to

225

her, how I could win her back. I would tell her that she was the love of my life, the absolute most wonderful person I'd ever met. I'd tell her that I still couldn't believe I got to wake up next to her every day — this gorgeous woman, this goddess. I would tell her that she was my one and only, my small darling, my bright spark in the darkness. And I'd promise to get better. To be better.

Onstage there was a blinding flash, and suddenly there stood beside the miser's bed a girl in a long white robe, a glowing tiara of lights and holly crowning her dark hair. She gazed solemnly at the quaking figure before her, eyes blazing with secret knowledge, too absorbed in her role to allow even the subtlest cheat to the audience to show them that she was just a human girl and not some avenging angel.

My daughter.

Are you the spirit whose coming was foretold to me?

I am!

Who, and what are you?

I am the Ghost of Christmas Past!

Long past?

No, my daughter intoned. *Your* past!

Tears sprang to my eyes. I watched transfixed as my daughter the ghost led her charge through the forgotten rooms of his past so he could see the shades of his former selves: the sad child at boarding school rescued by his favorite sister, the youth at a raucous Christmas Eve dance, the callow man dashing his beloved's naive hopes.

It was only a play, of course. Only little girls in too much makeup and homemade costumes, some more convincing than others as they moved awkwardly or fluidly around the stage, shouting out and sometimes stumbling over their lines, exaggerating their joy and grief so they could be more easily seen and understood.

It was only a play. But it was the ghost of Evie that I saw onstage, as if I were watching one of her pageants. And when we came to the happy family gathered around their holiday hearth, the smiling faces of the wife and children whom the miserable man was meant to treasure as his own, I began to weep openly.

Deep down, I knew my girls would be better off without me, just as my family had been better off without my father. They would be happy together, my wife and daughter — just the two of them, somewhere safe, somewhere apart from me, so that I couldn't bring us to ruin.

But how would they manage on their own? How would they survive? Couldn't they see that I labored day and night to be the best husband and father I could be? They had no idea how hard I tried for them, and it broke my heart.

I can still see it so clearly, that white-armed spirit flying around the stage. Sometimes, in my dreams, she flares up into flames. Other times, she holds my cold hands in hers, guiding me through my own show of shades.

But she never, ever speaks.

Leave me! the poor man howled. Take me back. Haunt me no longer!

These are the shadows of things that have been, my daughter cried. That they are what they are — do not blame me!

They grappled, until finally the wretch tackled my girl with a heavy blanket, putting out her light and plunging the rest of us into darkness.

When it was all over — the miser redeemed, the Christmas spirit victorious, the girls linking arms and bowing to waves of screams until the curtains closed around them — I roused myself from the back row and went in search of my wife. The auditorium felt like a train station at rush hour, everyone dawdling in their rows with their coats slung over their arms, clutching paper-wrapped bouquets they'd bought from the PTA concessions table, waiting for their girls to emerge from backstage. I stepped out into the lobby and bought my own bouquet, shelling out ten dollars for a half dozen pink and white carnations that were already browning at their latticed edges.

These kinds of things mattered.

Finally, back inside, I spotted my wife. She was standing close to the stage, chatting with a trio of parents I did not know, two women and a well-dressed man. I watched her for a while, observing the way she behaved when she didn't know I could see her. She was animated, gesturing with her swan-wing hands; she was telling a story, courting everyone's gaze with a wantonness that I did not recognize. The man made some comment, and my wife touched his arm, tossing her head with laughter to reveal the porcelain pillar of her throat.

Then she looked up, and I swear I will never forget the way she seemed to flinch with her entire body, the way the light and cheer drained out of her face when she saw me there. I must have looked distraught, worn down by the trials of the day. That must have been why instead of waving me over to join her group, my wife quickly said her good-byes and moved away from her friends, coming up the aisle with her hands tucked into the pockets of her dark olive trench coat.

Hey, she said softly. I was afraid you hadn't come.

Of course I came, I said. I promised you I wouldn't miss it.

I know but —

But what?

I know it's been hard.

I wasn't ready to tell her about what had happened at work. Not now, and certainly not here. Instead, I slung my arm around her and drew her close to me.

Wasn't she amazing? I sighed. I couldn't believe that was our daughter up there.

My wife nodded, allowing her body to relax into mine.

She'll be so happy you were here to see her.

We stood like that for a while, holding each other quietly. I was lucky, so lucky to have this woman and child, so lucky to have this life, and the sense of inadequacy and disgrace that washed over me was so overwhelming that I almost began to weep again.

So what should we do to celebrate? I asked, trying to make my voice bright. I'd suggest ice cream, but she never wants any.

But my wife was shaking her head.

She's got plans already, remember?

What do you mean?

All of the girls are going out to the diner, and then she's spending the night at Chloe's house.

We didn't discuss this.

My wife coughed out a laugh, her eyes darting away from me, as if she were searching the room for someone else.

Of course we did, she said. I told you about it last week.

No you didn't.

You probably just forgot; you've been busy —

I wouldn't forget that, I insisted.

Then I don't know.

I've hardly seen her in weeks, and now I don't even get to see her tonight?

I'm sorry, I —

How could you do this to me?

Thomas, stop!

Mommy! Daddy!

There was our girl, dressed in her skinny jeans and Chuck Taylors and pink puffer coat but still made up like a doll — the pile of her dark hair still stiff with hair spray, her face a garish mask. She blitzed into our embrace, thrusting herself between our bodies and beaming up at us, welcoming

231

the downpour of our adulation.

You were incredible, darling!

Absolutely astonishing!

You liked it? She grinned with self-assurance, gripping her bouquet. You liked my scene?

It was the best part of the play.

Best part by far.

Olivia forgot one of her lines, but I stayed calm and made sure she didn't mess up the whole thing.

I guess you're a real professional.

Aren't you going to wash your face? Clean up?

You're not going out to the diner like that, are you?

Of course I am!

With all that makeup still on?

That's the whole point! It's tradition.

Her friends were converging on us now, a boisterous brigade of painted girls mobbing our little family. Before they could shear my daughter away from me, I pressed a twenty into her waiting palm.

Is that enough?

Yeah, I'm probably not going to eat that much.

Here, I said. Take another, just in case.

My wife pulled our girl into her, crushing her cheek against the rough wool of her coat and kissing her temple.

Text me when you get to Chloe's house.

Okay.

And don't stay up too late, I added. I don't want you getting sick again.

Okay. Take my flowers for me?

And then she was caught up in the swarm of her friends and carried away. Her voice joined the jungle racket of the other girls' mingled cries, their rouged mouths and blue-shadowed eyes like the bright feathers of birds. They streamed between us, a juggernaut of adolescence, separating me from my wife.

I looked over at her, trying to catch her eye over the din, trying to share a smile, to connect. But she didn't see me. She was staring at nothing, at no one — holding herself and rubbing her arms, as if they were sore.

At home, by unspoken agreement, we began to drink. Red wine for the lady, whiskey for yours truly. The house was cold, and for a while my wife wandered the downstairs rooms, putting the bouquet I'd bought into water and looking at things on her phone, still wearing her coat. Beau followed her anxiously. It was as if she had only stopped inside for a moment, as if she didn't intend

233

to stay for very long.

I built a fire, and when the larger logs caught and began to blaze I lay down on the living room sofa, the dog coiled up on the rug before me, close to the hearth. After a while my wife joined me, setting her phone and the vase of flowers on the coffee table next to our half-empty bottles. I lifted my legs to let her sit, and she let me lay them across her lap.

At first we didn't speak. We watched the flames, mesmerized by the blackening of the wood under tongues of tallow white.

So, she said finally, uncertainly.

What?

I'm guessing it didn't go well.

What makes you say that?

You haven't said a thing about it.

I told her everything. Almost everything. I told her it had been a brilliant idea, that I had been brilliant in my presentation, but that the executives hadn't understood — that they'd been short-sighted and scared, helpless under the thrall of their corporate overlords. I told her I had fought for what I believed, but that even my efforts to take a principled stand had been misinterpreted and decried. I told her I was still proud of the work I'd done, that nothing would ever change that, no matter what happened to me now.

I didn't tell her anything about Carly and Abigail's initial doubts, and certainly nothing about their ultimate vindication. I didn't tell her about the cruel laughter in the conference room — laughter at *my* expense — or the exact words I'd used to defend myself. I didn't tell her about Greg's anger, or any of what he'd said when he sent me away. My fears about my job. None of that was part of my story.

When I finished, my wife took my hands in hers.

Oh, Thomas. I'm so sorry.

I shrugged. I didn't want her to see how full of shame and concern I really was, how low I felt. What good could come of that?

Well, things will either get better or get worse, I said dismissively. There's nothing I can do about it now.

Right, she said. So don't worry about it.

She was getting tipsy now, loose from all the wine, her tongue rough and dark with it. She wriggled out from under my legs and sank down on top of me, draping her body over mine, her bent knees wedged between my thighs. Our voices turned silken, our words dreamlike.

What are you doing?

What do you mean?

You're being very —

What?

Amorous.

So? You don't like it?

I didn't say that.

This was exactly what I wanted, exactly what I needed. What we needed. I stroked my wife's hair, gently ran my hands up and down her back. She nuzzled her face into my chest, and when she spoke again I felt her mouth moving against my ribs.

Do you remember when we met?

Of course, I said. (So she was feeling sentimental too, then.) Of course I remember. I couldn't believe you were there on my corner.

She laughed softly. It was a lucky choice, that bar, she said.

You were the most radiant woman I'd ever seen.

That's right, she sighed. You even liked me more than Mathilde. *That* had never happened before. Men were always more attracted to her.

She was touching me now, tracing the row of buttons on my shirt, but something didn't feel right. It was something about what she was saying. I sat up, disentangling myself, letting her body slide heavily onto the sofa beside me.

What are you talking about?

She regarded me vaguely. I always knew when she was very drunk because the whites of her eyes would flush pink, like spit-out toothpaste streaked with blood.

You don't remember?

I remember I found you at the bar on my corner.

Yes. And I was there with my friends, Mathilde and Camille and Anne-Laure. We were all on holiday together. Remember? You flirted with all of us, but in the end you picked me out of the group and whisked me away, even though I was trying to read my book the whole time. You said I was the signal in the noise.

I still try to remember it that way, even now. I see myself in the dark mahogany ark of the inn, see the ruby and saffron chevrons of the stained glass windows, gone cloudy from the cold outside and all the hot breath within. I see a cluster of women gathered around the bend of the broad wooden bar, their bodies a shifting collage of hips and shoulders, legs crossed to reveal a shapely haunch on a high stool. They are laughing, their voices echoing against the high tin ceiling as I wade into their perfumed midst.

And then I see her. That dark cloud of hair, that long and slender neck. That striking, unforgettable face. She's small and bright, a spark in the darkness, a quavering light that I long to shield and defend.

The women around her dissolve. She alone is insoluble.

But that wasn't the way it happened. Those are just more borrowed images, more invented memories. Someone else's story.

No, I said. No. You were there alone.

No I wasn't. I never traveled by myself.

Then why did you come home with me that night? Why did you spend that whole week with me?

Because I was a very young and very silly girl, and you were very charming and persuasive once you had set your sights on me, she said. And at the time, I thought winning you was a great victory. I thought it was all very romantic. That's the sort of thing the girls and I always used to do on those trips.

What?

Go home with men. Let them pay for things.

I was stunned. For a long moment I couldn't think of anything to say. I watched my wife watch the fire, wondering who she was. I looked at her left hand in her lap and saw that she wasn't wearing her engagement ring anymore. Maybe she hadn't worn it for a long time.

You never told me about this, I said finally, but she was shaking her head.

I've told you all about this, many times. You used to like hearing about it — all about my adventures — but now you can't stand the thought of it.

Of what?

Of me ever being with anyone else. Of me being independent.

Why do you always do this?

Do what?

You always turn everything into a fight.

She was silent then, staring into the flames, shrinking into herself.

You stayed with me, I said. You wanted to stay. You chose me.

You convinced me to stay, she said. You made all kinds of promises about how wonderful everything would be, and I let myself be convinced. I didn't know what it would really be like. How normal. How dull.

You really think that's what happened?

Yes.

Well, I don't know then, I said. I don't know what you're saying, and I have no idea why you're saying it now.

I don't know either, she said, getting up. Never mind.

Unless you're saying all of this just to hurt

me, I said. That's always a possibility.

Just forget it, she said. Don't listen to me.

She lay down on the floor, close to the blaze, her body a dark mound curled beside the dog.

What are you doing?

I'm cold.

Oh come on, Miri, I said. Don't be like this.

Come here, Beau, she murmured, reaching out to fondle the dog's curly mane. Good boy, good boy *mon petit chou. Mon ami.* Come here.

But the dog wouldn't stay with her. He was alert now, pacing and whimpering with inarticulate need.

What is it? I asked. What is it?

I took him outside. The backyard was quiet, our trees and bushes coated with cold white clumps, as if painted thickly with white primer, the black sky overhead pricked with stars.

Things will either get better or worse, I thought. *There's nothing I can do about it now.* I didn't really mean that, did I? Wasn't there always something else that could be done? I would have to find a way. I would. I always did.

The dog shuffled thoughtfully around the yard, lifting his hind leg to mark the places that needed to be marked.

When I came back inside I found the charred remains of my bouquet cast into the dying fire, stems writhing over the logs like gray worms. My wife was asleep on the floor, breathing hoarsely and haltingly, her head cradled in her arms.

Miri, I said. Sweetheart.

She didn't respond.

This wasn't the way the evening was supposed to go. This wasn't what I'd wanted, or what I'd envisioned. I knew that it was pointless to try mending what couldn't be mended. But I wondered if I should wake her so that we could make up, hold and forgive each other. It was what we used to do, whenever things were tough — absolving each other through the lucid language of our bodies — but lately we'd let too many nights rot into silence and recrimination.

And tonight it was especially necessary that we reconcile, because I realized that no matter how strong I was, and no matter how much the family depended on me to survive, I needed her. I needed her devotion in order to feel like myself again. I needed her to cry out and cling to me, helpless and senseless in my embrace. I needed confirmation that she would always be by my side.

Because I might lose everything else, but I

could never lose her.

I crouched down beside her, kneaded the soft flesh of her upper arm.

Miri. Wake up.

She moaned softly.

Miri. I shook her. Miri.

She moaned again, an incoherent syllable on her lips.

I hesitated for only a moment. Then I unsheathed her from the cable-knit skin of her sweater dress, using both hands to peel the garment over her hips and shoulders, releasing her from its casing. She sighed, moaned again. Then her woolen leggings, rolled down over her knees, abandoned with her cotton underwear in a knot at our feet.

Her body had changed over the years, corrupted by childbirth and age. It was no longer the body of the young woman I'd married. She was still reasonably slim, but her haunches had grown broad and mottled, riddled with tiny lumps. Her breasts had wilted, and her nipples were like raisins, shriveled and distended. There were bandages like railroad tracks down her spine, putty patches against her dusky skin. For what? I didn't know. I turned her over onto her back, her limbs heavy. Limp.

I can't remember much else from that night. My palm against her reddened cheek, maybe. My hands on her shoulders, my thumbs splayed against her clavicle.

Perhaps.

Maybe she began to moan — louder, more insistently — turning her head from side to side, her eyes still shut. Maybe she said my name. Maybe she begged me.

Maybe.

That's how it usually was. She'd always liked it that way, those kinds of games.

And when we woke at dawn — pale blue light glowing in the naked windows, the dog snuffing at our tender places — everything was fine.

The room had chilled again. My wife moved stiffly toward our bedroom, hugging herself, body bowed with cold and fatigue and the incipient aches of an oncoming hangover. Before I joined her, I tidied the living room, clearing away our bottles, straightening the rug where it had buckled and bunched around the legs of the coffee table, putting everything back in its place. Then I picked up my wife's phone.

It sounds invasive, I know. A violation. But over the past few months I'd grown so accustomed to checking devices, constantly monitoring my daughter's internet usage to make sure she wasn't getting into trouble again, that casual surveillance had become second nature. My daughter had earned back her own phone with texting privileges over Thanksgiving, but she still used my wife's phone sometimes, browsing online boutiques and playing music videos in the passenger seat of the car or at the kitchen island while dinner was prepared.

But if I'm being honest, that wasn't even why I checked. I don't know what I was looking for. It may have been wrong, but it was unconscious, my fingers working of their own accord to type in my wife's passcode and scroll through her messages and history.

It's pointless for me to describe what I found, what I saw. All those messages in French to people I didn't know. The details don't matter, certainly not anymore. I know that cataloging those simple facts might show something of the life she was living — the sliver of her life that excluded me — but I also know that it would fail to add up to anything that could possibly explain the inexplicable.

It was nothing, really.

Other men may have faced their suspicions head-on. They may have confronted their wives, asking questions, demanding explanations. They may have raged through their houses, extorting tearful apologies, hounding their women into meek submission.

But I would never do anything like that. I wasn't that kind of man.

Besides, it was nothing.

The following Friday the first shipment of Christmas presents arrived; I found them waiting for me on the front porch when I came home from work.

It had been a tense and exhausting week, my subordinates giving me a wide berth, Greg throwing around ominous words like *accountability* and *probation* when he deigned to speak with me. I had a few small, new projects — fewer and smaller than I'd expected — and I was struggling to begin meaningful work on any of them. Nothing had been said about my bonus, or my raise, or about anything else coming up after the New Year.

The girls were still out. My daughter must have been at some kind of lesson, but who knows what my wife was doing, or where she was. Maybe with friends I didn't know. Maybe alone at a bar. Maybe sitting in her car, tapping out more of those messages, her fingers tickling and stroking her screen.

There were several packages stacked on the porch. Most of what I'd ordered was for the girls, but there was one item I'd ordered for myself, something that had caught my eye during my late-night browsing: a simple piece from a craftsman in War Eagle. It was something I realized I'd wanted for a while, my own talisman for today. As soon as I'd seen the product photo — red cedar posed on a brick mantel — I'd been able to feel the club's reassuring heft in my hands, and as soon as I'd clicked Buy It Now I'd already felt more secure. More in control.

The falling snow had silenced our street. I stood on the porch for a while in the thickening dark, surveying the precarious pile, this bulwark that shielded our threshold. Then I knelt, gathered the boxes in my arms, and carried them into the house.

IV

Dawn in the valley, a distant sound of bells.

The first pale blue of the day reveals the hidden shape of the mountains, still black against the new light. A young shepherd sings a song to the goddess of spring and plays his pipe, his tune by turns jaunty and mournful.

A lost and lonely traveler awakens, sprawled in dew-soaked grass. He is surprised to find himself there, safe and alive, as though he has survived a shipwreck. Indeed he has, in a manner of speaking. At the very last moment, he chose to leave an underworld of erotic reverie and return to the world of mortals, leaving the sins of his past behind. Now he hears the song of pilgrims traveling through the rifts and ridges of the vale. They approach, exhausted yet euphoric, their voices soft at first, then swelling over the solitary music of the shepherd boy and his pipe.

The traveler stands stunned for a moment. Then, overcome with gratitude, he falls to his knees, and the chorus of the pilgrims overwhelms the pastoral scene. The traveler takes up their song, praising God for his deliverance, his own voice rising up to heaven.

Then a harsh clap of static, a deafening pop against the ear.

Sorry!

My daughter tiptoes barefoot from the kitchen into the dining room, her arms spread like wings, her wrists bent, her fingertips splayed — a performance of exaggerated care.

There was something wrong with the stereo receiver. If you moved around the downstairs of the house with too heavy a tread the signal would fade, voices drowned by a rush of garbled buzzing.

Daddy, why does it keep doing that?

It's doing that because of all the other electronics in the house, like your cell phone. They're interfering with the reception.

That's crazy. I don't believe that.

Just don't move around so much, okay?

When is this going to be over?

It just started.

Ugh, *really*?

You know, sweetheart, many people are of the opinion that this is the greatest opera ever written.

So?

So just listen.

We are listening to — or rather, *trying* to listen to — the Met's Saturday live radio broadcast of *Tannhäuser*. It is Saturday, April 13, the first unseasonably warm weekend of the year. Outside, purple and periwinkle crocuses adorn the dirt along the driveway, and the yellow heads of the daffodils are beginning to peer out from their slim paper bag sheaths. There is a heavy stillness in the unaccustomed heat, a buzz of insects in the air. Light and moisture hover like a beaded curtain, golden and solid. The first promise of summer, the good seasons still before us.

But we don't get to enjoy the beautiful day. My girls and I are inside, ranged around the dining room table, absorbed in the creation of a school project. Spread before us is a pizza box that we have transformed into a topographical map, a board game charting Buck's journey through the Yukon in *The Call of the Wild*.

My wife has become fixated on painting the crags and plateaus of each papier-mâché snow-capped mountain, dabbing their flanks with varying shades of blue and green to heighten their sense of depth, texture, and shadow. My daughter busies herself fashioning tiny animals out of clay — wolfish dogs, doggish wolves, lumbering bears and seals. The girls labor quietly, their faces peaceful in concentration, like angels in a medieval fresco, or two of Vermeer's maids bent over their sewing in the window light. I'm making the playing cards:

Stolen from Judge Miller — Lose a turn

Defeat Spitz — Move forward 3 spaces and earn 3 tokens

Adopted by Thornton — Earn 2 tokens

Law of the Club — Go back 3 spaces

It has been well documented in numerous accounts of April 13 that the temperature would plummet forty degrees by nightfall, after I had dropped off my daughter at the old house where I grew up for a long-promised evening of movies and takeout with her grandmother and aunts. By midnight it would be snowing. Almost every article and official report makes note of this curious fact, as if the freakish shift from summer to winter that night was a sign of something more meaningful than just a particularly powerful cold front.

No, the schizophrenic weather meant absolutely nothing, but if any of these media or law enforcement philistines had even the slightest passing knowledge of opera or art, they might have noted the poetic irony of the Met's *Tannhäuser* radio broadcast that day. The title character is the perfect anti-hero — noble and good-hearted, yet catastrophically impulsive in his emotions. The opera is irresistible in its scope, ingenious in the way it elevates the human drama of relationships to a struggle between salvation and damnation — a battle between our base, egotistical urges and our relentless pursuit of purity. These are the struggles we all face in our dealings with the ones we love.

I have said before that I believe I share a strong affinity with Tannhäuser. I see myself in him, even as I question his choices. Why does he publicly admit to the crimes of his past when his world has already taken him back with open arms? Why does he throw it all away once more?

The truth is that it had to be that way. They all would have found out eventually. Elisabeth, his virginal true love — she would have found out. And then what would have become of him? No, he had to confess, and he had to suffer the terrible pains of the road that lay ahead. He had to lose what he loved most. His abnegation was the only way for him to be saved.

And this, in the end, is why I must tell this story: because only a public reckoning of what I have done could ever possibly absolve me.

But first, the shooting.

On a Thursday morning in March, a middle-aged man armed with two assault rifles, a family heirloom Winchester, and a kitchen knife walked through the service entrance of the Saint Perpetua School for Girls on East Ninety-first Street, where his estranged wife worked in the finance office. Shortly after entering the building, the gunman was confronted by a sixty-two-year-old security guard, a Trinidadian gentleman who was just four months from retirement. It was second period, the hallways empty. The gunman shot the security guard in the face, then barricaded himself in the nearest ground-floor classroom, taking twenty-one fourth graders and their two teachers as his hostages. Shouting through the door, he demanded to speak to his wife, who had just started the process of divorcing him.

Three hours into the standoff, the gunman executed the head teacher, a mother of twin boys who had taught at the school for almost two decades. About an hour later, the gunman killed the assistant teacher, a young woman who was an alumna of Saint Perpetua and had recently gotten engaged.

It is difficult to imagine what happened after that — what it was like in that bloody room for those poor girls. Supposedly the gunman insisted they sing pop songs, that they take turns as soloists. He told them to think of the whole thing as an adventure, a story to tell their own daughters one day. He was still sure his demands would be met and that the rest of them could go home safely.

He would have mercy on them.

I imagine the girls, gripped with terror in the familiar surroundings of their classroom, sitting cross-legged on the rug and staring up at the face of the lethargic clock, the black-and-white grid of their construction-paper silhouette self-portraits, the diagram of the water cycle, and the yellowed reproduction of the Declaration of Independence — all of it incomprehensible and alien, mysterious texts unearthed from a long-forgotten culture. None of it could help them now.

Negotiations broke down. The gunman executed two girls with single shots to the back of their heads before the SWAT team could break down the door. Another three girls were killed in the brief gun battle that followed.

We watched it unfold at the office. After the first breaking-news alert dinged our phones, someone turned on the television in the main lounge on the second floor, and all of us who didn't need to be anywhere else gathered around to stare at the footage playing out on the screen, periodically checking the small screens in our hands for identical coverage. There were aerial views of the police cordon that had been erected around Saint Perpetua, pointless interviews with unconnected pedestrians, grim analysis from experts and talking heads. We watched it all, unable to look away. Greg poked his head in, saw that some women in the room were weeping.

I can't deal with this right now, he said. He walked out.

Others, chastened, followed him back to work. Abigail had begun to sob, snuffling into her hands. Without thinking, I sat beside her and patted her shoulder in an avuncular gesture of commiseration, murmured something comforting as the room emptied around us.

It's just so awful, she moaned.

I know, I said. It's unimaginable.

How could someone do that?

I don't know.

Evil. It's just evil.

Her flushed face felt hot beside mine. I moved my hand from her shoulder to her knee, rubbed the soft mound of it consolingly.

After work we went to our usual happy hour bar. I ordered two Laphroaigs for us, followed Abigail's lead when she downed hers in one hard swallow.

Easy, kid.

Ha, she barked, wiping her plump mouth with the back of her wrist. So I'm a kid now?

You've always been a kid.

Oh please. Just get us another round.

We got drunk. The night became reduced, dark and slow, boiled down to isolated images: Abigail crying, Abigail laughing, Abigail licking her lips and sticking out her tongue. Abigail's knee wedged between mine. Abigail leaning her heavy torso over the dark wood of the bar, her fingers raised in a crooked peace sign as she signaled for another round.

I got home somehow. Late. I don't recall speaking with my wife, though I must have. She would have been upset about the shooting too.

The Saint Perpetua massacre troubled everyone. How could it not? Some people fret that with each new act of annihilation the public grows a bit more jaded, a bit less able to feel, but this one was different, somehow. The outpouring of grief was national in scale. Small towns all over erected memorials, planting octets of wooden angels in public squares. The president wept at a televised vigil. Charity drives were initiated and fully funded within days. Comfort dogs padded through the halls of the city's schools. The governor of New York attended each of the victim's funerals, was photographed clasping the hands of bereaved parents on the steps of Saint Patrick's Cathedral as raindrops slicked the shoulders of his dark suit.

Even so, even as the city and nation performed their rites of collective mourning, the weight of the tragedy felt especially onerous to me, as if its particularities had singled me out for suffering.

I couldn't sleep. When I did sleep, I had nightmares. My daughter's voice calling for me as I ran through a labyrinth of locker-lined hallways. A faceless figure behind a glass door, pounding and pounding, demanding to be let in. The governor of New York questioning me, asking me what I knew.

I couldn't talk to my wife or my daughter

about any of it. I didn't want to upset them by forcing them to engage with my private horrors. Saint Perpetua was too much like Hutch; the tragedy had struck too close to home, and its reverberations rattled too close to our comfortable life. It was a reminder of everything I was powerless to prevent.

That's when my night drives began. Around midnight, after the girls had gone to sleep, I would leave the house and drive to the vast, empty field of the mall parking lot, where the orderly painted rectangles glowed like farm plots under the moon of the streetlight. There, I would make ceaseless circles. First slowly and deliberately, as if looking for a parking spot, then as fast as I could gun the engine, racing myself around and around the lot. I'd turn the radio up until the bass shook the car, until I couldn't even hear the music, my hands vibrating on the wheel. As the night streaked nauseatingly against my windows, I would grind my molars together until they squeaked and lean hard into each curve, and there would always be a moment in the turn when I felt so fast and weightless that I would almost lose control.

Thursday, April 11, a gray morning dampened by noncommittal rain. Just before nine a.m. a message whooshed into my in-box, alerting me that my attendance had been requested at a strategy meeting scheduled for two thirty that afternoon in the small conference room on the third floor. A good sign, I thought. Perhaps my probationary period was finally coming to an end. I accepted the invite and went about my day.

At 2:27 I went upstairs, a fresh coffee in hand and a pencil tucked behind my ear. As I strode down the hall, I may have wondered why the meeting was being held in this particular conference room — the windowless fishbowl with the frosted glass walls — when strategy meetings were usually held in one of the larger crystalline tanks below, but I probably didn't even register it.

I opened the door, and four silent faces turned to regard me. In the long moment that followed, I felt a chill slither down my sternum as I realized I did not know these people, save for a plain redheaded woman I thought I recognized from HR. The others were anonymous dark suits, positioned along either side of the conference table like pallbearers.

They had been waiting for me. They were not there for a strategy meeting.

The HR woman stood as I entered the

room. She wore a black blazer that I'm sure made her feel very powerful, heels higher than I would have expected. A flush of freckles in the folds of her neck. I did not know her name, could not bring it to mind.

Mr. Martin, she said. She did not smile, and she did not offer me her hand. Please join us.

Excuse me, I said. What is this?

The HR woman gestured to an empty chair across the table from her, nodding at it as if she agreed with something perceptive it had said.

Please, she said.

I sat; the HR woman sat. Now suits surrounded me — one on either side, two across, the four of them boxing me in. Who were these people? Management I'd never met? Lawyers? I didn't know them — didn't know their hometowns or alma maters or favorite teams. I didn't know anything about them.

On the table there were several pages of typed notes, ordered into two stacks. The print was upside down, facing away from me, too far away for me to decipher. When the HR woman saw me looking at the pages she drew them slightly closer to herself, then covered them with her folded hands. She cleared her throat.

We appreciate you being here, Mr. Martin.

Did I have a choice? I retorted. The HR woman ignored the remark, cleared her throat again.

I'll come right to the point, she said. Serious concerns about your conduct have been brought to our attention in recent days, and we need to address the accusations with you before proceeding.

Before proceeding with what? I demanded. What accusations?

Mr. Martin, please. You are familiar with Ms. Abigail Landry?

Abigail licking her lips. Abigail laughing. Abigail wriggling, Abigail unbuttoning. Abigail crying. A wave of nausea rocked through me, roiling my gut.

Yes, I said. I know her.

Ms. Landry has filed an extensively documented complaint against you alleging a long-standing pattern of sexual harassment and assault.

All sound left the room. I watched the HR woman's mouth moving, but could not hear what she was saying. I swallowed hard and the sound came back.

Central to Ms. Landry's complaint is an evening this past December, shortly before the holidays, the HR woman was saying.

Ms. Landry maintains that, after working very late on an important presentation, you pressured her to drink until she blacked out. She contends that you then coerced her into performing sexual acts on you, and that you only allowed her to stop when she became physically incapacitated and could no longer move.

I thought back to that night, remembered Abigail draping herself over me, remembered her rubbing her body against mine, unbuttoning my fly. There had been no coercion — she had insisted, and I had refused. That was how I remembered it.

That's not what happened, I said finally. I know what you're talking about, and that is not at all what happened that night.

I'm afraid that's not the only incident in the complaint. Ms. Landry has recorded a number of incidents over the course of the last two years.

That's not possible.

Do you recall anything about the company Christmas party the year Ms. Landry was hired?

No.

Or taking her home in a car service one night last June?

No. No, of course I don't remember that. None of this makes any sense.

Ms. Landry maintains that you consistently pressure her to stay late and drink with you, and that you yourself frequently drink to excess in her company.

That's not true.

She says that when you drink you become physical with her, and she feels obligated to respond to your sexual advances because she fears you will become violent and vindictive if she does not.

No.

She says your behavior creates a hostile work environment and has caused her acute physical and psychological distress. She is afraid to come to work and has confessed to self-harm and suicidal ideation.

It was a story fit for a failed writer like Abigail, a sordid and predictable piece of garbage. I couldn't believe she had the balls to share it with the public.

But this is completely unfounded, I protested. This is a classic case of her word against mine. It doesn't mean anything.

Mrs. Bloom also supports Ms. Landry's version of events. She coauthored all the documentation dating back over the last six months.

I looked down at the pages again, trying to read them, to see what they said about me and what I had done. What I had allegedly done.

May I see them? I asked. The notes?

I'm afraid that's not possible.

Then I want to speak to Carly. Mrs. Bloom, I mean.

I'm sorry, Mr. Martin. As you know, Mrs. Bloom is on maternity leave, and in any case, I highly doubt her attorney would allow any direct contact at this stage.

Well why aren't we having a mediation? I asked. Isn't that how these things usually work? Don't I get to face my accuser?

Ms. Landry and her attorney felt she might be in danger.

Oh, bullshit! I've been nothing but a gentleman and mentor to Abigail — to Ms. Landry — ever since she was hired here.

That is not what the documentation shows.

But *she* came on to *me*! If anything I should be accusing *her* of misconduct.

Anyone could see that she wasn't my type at all — pasty, fattened with butter and grain. How had I ever entertained even a feigned attraction to that bloated chunk of flesh? She was nothing but trash from a cancerous, incestuous swamp. No wonder she'd decided to accuse me; I was a step up for her.

Mr. Martin, we understand that there can

be gray area, and that lines can be blurry. We know stories can change based on who tells them. But the documentation is so thorough — and there are witnesses too, you know. Unfortunately the pattern is impossible to ignore. And with everything happening in the industry now, management simply can't let these things slide.

Then why even bother talking to me about it?

The woman looked irritated then, a flash of disgust flitting into her eyes before she could stop it.

If there were specific evidence to exonerate you, then we may have been able to come to a different conclusion, she said, an edge to her voice now. However, that does not seem to be the case. In any event, we were legally obligated to speak to you before proceeding with termination.

I blinked.

I'm fired?

Yes, Mr. Martin. We are terminating your employment, as of today.

A very long pause.

We also suggest you retain a lawyer. That is if you don't already have one, the woman added. There are some firms we can recommend, if you'd like.

I'll admit it, I almost laughed then. They

were being totally irrational, completely delusional. After everything I'd done for this firm, they couldn't do this to me.

Where's Greg? I asked. I want to see Greg. He should be here for this.

Mr. Conroy accepts the decision of human resources, and seeks to avoid exposing the firm to any further threat of legal action. He will not be involving himself any more than he already has.

Suddenly it had become difficult to breathe. I had wanted to deny these suits the satisfaction of a hysterical response, but now I knew that would be impossible. Sweat soaked my shirt. A buzzing had begun in my left ear, and as I sat there the sound sharpened to a piercing shriek, a needle in my skull. I had been abandoned and betrayed, hung out to dry. This wasn't supposed to happen.

Mr. Martin, are you in need of assistance?

They were all gawking at me. Vultures, waiting for me to collapse so they could pick over my corpse and take whatever was left. I let out one long shudder of a sigh, passed my hand over my face.

No, I said finally. No, thank you. I don't need anything.

I took almost nothing from my office. Just the photographs of the girls, the art that my daughter had made for me. *I LovE DAdy.*

If this were a movie, I would have seen Abigail on my way out of the office for the last time. I would have caught sight of her behind the protective glass of a conference room, would have seen her red-faced, hiccupping with coloratura sobs as she milked her moment. The other women in the firm would surround her in sisterly solidarity, and they would lay their hands on her doughy limbs, propping her up and propelling her into what they promised would be a better future. She would stay, and I would go.

Fat bitch. Whore.

But I didn't see her. I walked out without seeing anyone, without anyone saying anything to me. Then I was enclosed in the metal sarcophagus of the elevator, sinking to the earth. And finally I was out on the street, squinting into the heavy white sky of the overcast afternoon.

Maybe I deserved it. Maybe this was my comeuppance, my punishment for the manifold ways I had failed over the years as a husband and father. There had been too many late nights, too much time that should have been spent with the girls that I had sacrificed at the altar of my own selfish striving.

And for what? What had my sacrifice brought me, aside from ruin? Just like Tannhäuser, I had taken my position for granted, and because of my hubris I had been cast out of the grand halls where I once thrived, banished to seek atonement for my alleged sins. But how could I possibly atone now?

Everything had been taken from me.

On the drive home I thought about what to tell my wife. Certainly I didn't have to tell her everything. I would not tell her about Abigail's accusations, or anything about the things I had allegedly done. Emphasis on the allegedly, of course. But I would have to tell her I had lost my job. There was no getting around that, no hiding it from her.

Could I tell her I had been fired without explaining why? Treat my termination as an act of God, an unforeseen challenge that, while catastrophic, we would overcome together? *Things will either get better or worse. There's nothing you can do about it now, so don't worry.* That's what she told me months ago, consoling me when I doubted myself. Maybe she could console me now, even though I had wrecked both of our lives.

It was dusk now, the street washed with shadows. As I rumbled down our gravel

267

drive and approached the house I could see my wife framed in the kitchen window. I beheld her profile — her dark bowed head, her downward gaze absorbed by the laptop screen before her — and felt a surge of admiration for the beauty of her form. She had the warmth of a mother in a Cassatt, the elegance of an aristocrat in a Sargent — she always looked like a painting.

Should I tell her now and get it over with? Or wait until our daughter was in bed and I had opened another bottle of wine? Wait until we were holding each other tenderly on the sofa, the way we used to when we were young?

Get it over with, I decided.

My keys rattled in my hand as I opened the side door and stepped into the kitchen. My wife turned and looked up at me, quick fingertip closing the browser window on the screen, her face brightening into a loving smile.

How was your day, darling?

And in that moment I knew I couldn't tell her. I just couldn't. Not right then. Not even that night. Instead I took her in my arms, pulling her backward against my chest with a passionate spontaneity that made her gasp, then laugh.

My day? I murmured, kissing her neck. It

was fine.

Anything new?

I held her closer and shut my eyes, listened to the pulse beating in her throat.

No, I said. Nothing to report.

And then she began to chatter on about the little events of her own day, and I knew I was safe. For the time being, at least.

The next morning was like any other weekday morning. I woke up at five thirty and ran a brisk five-mile loop around the sleeping neighborhood — the cold white streetlights still burning, the lawns glimmering with dew, the sounds of my huffed breaths and pounding tread imposing a dogged rhythm on the silent dawn. Another overcast day, rain threatening. Then home again, a hot shower. Brewed coffee in the Chemex as the house began to stir. Two hard-boiled eggs, an apple, a tablespoon of almond butter — all of it eaten standing at the kitchen counter. I could hear my wife upstairs, pleading with my daughter to get up. Then the sputter and hush of the shower turned on, the stamped feet of an exhausted adolescent. The dog crouched below me, waiting for dropped morsels, sniffing the air expectantly. I scanned the day's headlines on my phone: sarin gas attacks in Gaza, the secretary of state indicted for enslaving his housekeeper. On the radio, the ardent trio from the first scene of *Don Giovanni* (furious father, disgraced daughter, callow Casanova) — *do not hope, unless you kill me, that I shall ever let you run away.*

Then my wife was downstairs, standing before me in her bare feet and the silk robe that I'd given her for her birthday last year, the one patterned with pale coral peonies. Her dark hair looked mussed and warm, and she smiled drowsily at me, her eyes still squinted with sleep. Just like any other weekday morning.

What time will you be home tonight?

The usual time, I said quickly. Not too late.

Good. I'll make dinner.

That would be nice.

Why don't I roast a chicken? It's always so much better than the store-bought.

She was being so sweet to me, so loving and accommodating. A good wife.

I felt ill.

I've got to go, I said, armoring myself with my sports coat.

Already?

Got a client meeting first thing. Give our girl a kiss for me?

Of course. And one for me?

I stepped toward her. My wife closed her

eyes, tipped her face upward. Her soft mouth was pressed to mine for a suspended moment, and then I was out the door. I got in my car, backed out of the driveway, and drove toward the expressway that would take me to the city, just as I always did.

Except today I passed the bottleneck of station wagons and Suburbans turning onto the westbound entrance ramp, let the commuter traffic recede behind me. I loosened my tie, lifted it over my neck, and cast it onto the seat beside me. Then I followed the signs for the next entrance, eastbound.

I drove east until the highway sprawl of strip malls and car dealerships gave way to the green of farmland and pine barrens, drove until I reached the purer part of the island. There was a small white clapboard house a few miles past the end of the expressway that sold wonderful pies and other products made from the fruit they grew themselves. The girls and I had always bought provisions here when we spent the weekend out east, my wife being particularly partial to their boysenberry jam and fresh-pressed peach juice.

I pictured the three of us on one of these summer pilgrimages, my daughter in pale denim shorts, the heels of her bare feet propped against the backseat passenger-side window as she pouts into her phone, pivoting her head slightly to get the perfect shot, a pink tip of tongue protruding. My wife beside me, her jaw set in stoicism at the traffic, her oversize tortoiseshell sunglasses shielding her half-closed eyes.

I stopped at the little store and spent twenty-six dollars on a blackberry apple pie, picked at its flushed and glutinous innards with a plastic spoon I found in the glove compartment while sitting alone in the parking lot.

For the rest of the day I traversed the country roads of the North Fork, seeking out familiar landmarks. There was the roadside shack where my daughter had made a delighted mess cracking the claws of her first lobster; the bed-and-breakfast where the girls and I had once stayed, the one with the chickens and goats in the backyard; the vineyards my wife refused to patronize, insisting they would insult her sophisticated French palate; all the quaintly moldering towns named for Indian tribes our government had long ago decimated through disease and development. Midweek in the low season it seemed I could go for miles without encountering another car, but in another month or so these abandoned roads and quiet towns would be congested with the cars of vacationing families just like mine.

Would we ever be able to count ourselves among them again?

Late in the afternoon I got back on the expressway and headed west. It was still too early to go home, so I took the exit for the Ocean Parkway and crossed the bridge over the bay to the beach. The lot was deserted, the sea matte gray under a matte gray sky, deep hollows carved into the shore by the series of almost weekly nor'easters we'd had that spring. I walked along the surf for a while, watching for the black marks of boats on the barely perceptible horizon as seagulls shrieked overhead.

Then I got back into the car. I read the news on my phone until it died and the screen went black. I may have fallen asleep — at some point I may have sobbed, my forehead pressed to the steering wheel — but in all honesty I can't remember what else I did, how I passed the time until the evening.

I do remember that I had to throw out the rest of the pie — it was my wife's favorite kind, the blackberry apple, but I couldn't possibly bring it back with me.

I went home. Once again I rumbled down

the gravel drive, once again I could see my wife framed in the kitchen window as I approached the house. Once again I hesitated at the side door before going in, keys awkward in my hand. The kitchen was warm and inviting, rich with the smells of chicken fat and rosemary. My wife received me with a soft kiss and a glass of red wine, then turned back to the oven to check on the root vegetables roasting beneath the bird. A good wife, a truly good wife. A perfect picture of happiness. It was everything I had ever wanted, but now I couldn't shake the feeling that I was merely a visitor in a dream — that I was living someone else's life.

How was your day, darling?

Oh fine, I sighed, settling myself at the counter and sifting distractedly through the bills that had come in the mail. Hutch tuition. Electric. Amex. Home insurance.

And your meeting?

What meeting?

The one you told me about this morning.

I had forgotten. For several sickening seconds I struggled to invent something, *anything,* but after decades of experience spinning stories not even the flimsiest imaginary client or fictional pitch would come to mind. Not now, when I needed it most.

I was rescued by my daughter, who chose that moment to come marching down the stairs. I had expected her to greet me with her usual elation at my homecoming, but this evening she looked grim, all bitten lip and huffed breath. She and my wife exchanged a sharp look, a current of resentment passing between them.

What's wrong, sweetheart? I asked, my voice light and even, grateful for the interruption. My daughter pushed herself into my arms and looked at my wife again, who turned away, shaking her head.

Does Daddy know?

I haven't told him anything, my wife replied tersely, focusing her gaze on the cucumbers she was now slicing for the salad. You have to tell him.

But *Mommy* —

You tell him!

My daughter sighed heavily, then pressed her cheek against my chest, her voice lowering to a baby-voiced whimper.

I have a big project to do on *The Call of the Wild,* she whispered as I stroked her hair.

All right.

I have to make a board game. And write an essay.

Okay.

And they're due on Monday.

Okay.

And I haven't started yet.

My wife sighed and threw up her hands in exasperation as my daughter cowered against me.

Oh come on, I said. You're not helping.

How is it possible that the project is due on Monday and she hasn't even started?

My wife and daughter began to bicker, but I couldn't follow what they were saying. Couldn't hear them. The relief I had felt at the change of subject had given way to a debilitating sense of impotence. Of deafness. There was that buzzing in my ear again, canceling out all other sound. It was as if I were far away, watching the girls from a high window, my hands pressed against the thick glass that silenced the world below. My life would go on without me.

Stop it, I said finally. Just stop.

The girls lapsed into bitter silence.

We'll get it done, I added, even though I had no idea how we would. We have all weekend to work on it.

What about movie night?

Movie night?

At Grandma's house. With Deedee and Kit. I'm supposed to go tomorrow night.

Forget about it, my wife spat. You're not going.

Mommy.

You have to learn to take responsibility for yourself.

She can still go, I said. Since when are you so hard on her?

Since when do you spoil her?

A timer went off. My wife took the chicken out of the oven and set it on the counter before me with more force than she needed to.

We can eat now, she said. Everything is ready.

Wonderful, I said, trying to restore the sense of tenderness that had marked my arrival. It looks delicious.

I don't want any chicken, my daughter whined.

I don't care, my wife retorted. It's what we're having.

I won't eat it.

Then you can starve to death.

I wish I would.

That night I lay awake for what felt like hours, heartsick and afraid. My wife lay beside me, sleeping soundly — though her face was turned away from mine, each of her subtle stirrings snapped me further into wakefulness. I stared up at the blank of the ceiling, turned to see the red glow of the digital alarm clock bleeding onto the wall.

Giving up on sleep, I crept out of bed and left the house, sighing with relief once I had returned to the safe and sterile capsule of my car. Without thinking, I drove the familiar route to the mall, ready to circle the parking lot until I lost all sense of myself.

But tonight there was another car parked in my arena: a decade-old beige Honda Accord, its rear bumper plastered with simpering slogans of corporate liberalism: *Coexist. Hope Anchors the Soul. Take Back the Night.* It sat there on the edge of the lot, almost beyond the streetlight's glow.

What was it doing there? Perhaps housing a high school tryst, or a lone weed smoker. Someone else who wanted to be alone.

No matter. I began to make my circles, slowly at first, then faster and faster, until the sky spun around me. I had no intention of disturbing the sanctimonious Honda or its occupant — I wasn't crazy or disturbed. It just happened to be in my path.

As I roared past the car for the third time, nearly clipping its side view mirror, someone rolled down the window and cried out after me.

Slow the fuck down! I'm calling the police!

I should have left then. I should have driven away. I should have gone home, where I could still pretend I belonged. I know I shouldn't have done what I did next.

But I did it.

I stomped on the brakes and sent my car into shrieking reverse, barreling backward until I was face-to-face with this idiot — this girl, as it turned out. In a brief moment I took in her blond bangs, her bloated face, her NYU sweatshirt.

It was as if the specter of Abigail had come to taunt me — my own fat, whorish Ghost of Christmas Past.

Not long past. My past.

I'm calling the police, the girl repeated, her voice and hand trembling as she held up her phone, as if to prove to me that she was indeed serious.

Go ahead, I snarled.

Dialing, she didn't notice me unbuckle my seatbelt, didn't notice me get out of my car. Too late, she looked up and realized I was beside her, my body pressed against her door.

Then my head and torso had breached the boundary of her open window, and in one smooth gesture I had snatched the phone out of her hand, hurling it like a discus into the vast and empty lot.

Then I began to scream.

In all honesty I have no memory of what I said, or if I said anything at all. Maybe I was just howling and grunting, making animal noises. All I can remember is the girl's expression as she pressed herself to the opposite window, as far away from me as she could get. I remember her abject fear, her paralysis — as if she saw a version of me that no one else could see.

I suppose I just wanted to scare her. I kept her captive for a while, banging on her roof with my fists, thrusting my pelvis against her door, listening as her whimpers turned into sobs. It was as if I had forgotten who I was.

Finally I leaned in even closer — close enough to kiss her — and spit in her face. Then I got back in my car and peeled out of the lot.

When I finally returned to my dark and silent house I sat in the driveway for a long time before going inside. I climbed the stairs and watched the sleeping forms of the girls in their beds — first my daughter, then my wife. They were just shapes under their blankets, breathing.

They could have been anyone.

You're probably wondering what my plan was. When I would confess. I knew I couldn't keep it up forever, this hiding and lying.

But the truth is I had no plan. All I knew was that the weekend seemed like a safe time to talk. My wife and I would wake up late, for once, and lie together as long as we could, before the demands of daughter and dog forced us to get out of bed. We always treasured those rare moments that we had to ourselves: the toes of her left foot tucked between my ankles, the warm weight of my hand on hers, so familiar that it was almost imperceptible, a breeze through the half-open window, sun mottling the wall behind our heads. I wouldn't have to jam my explanations into the margins of routine; there would be no daily stresses to infringe upon what needed to be said.

It was supposed to be a gorgeous day, finally — the first really warm day of the long-awaited spring. My wife and I would sit together on our front porch and talk about the future, figure things out. I could help her understand. I could soothe her, make my words right, promise her that everything would turn out fine for us in the end.

I just hadn't counted on the school project.

Let's see us again, that day.

I remember the three of us working together in the dining room.

I remember sun streaming through the venetian blinds onto the table, slices of light cutting over ill-formed papier-mâché mountains.

I remember the vase of orange tulips, four days in water, opening their petals to reveal the black dust within.

I remember Beau poking around at our ankles, looking for edible morsels as always. He must have eaten something bad the night before, because early that morning he had vomited a thin yellow gruel onto my daughter's bed. Now her duvet cover was in the wash, the rhythmic bump of the dryer balls like the beat of a frightened heart as the laundry tumbled over and over.

I remember my wife, sun on her dark hair as she bent over her work. I remember pausing behind her to knead her shoulders, my palms absorbing the warmth of her skin under her sheer cotton shirt. I remember her moving around the room humming, watercolor brush like a conductor's baton in her hand, a lightness and looseness in her gestures that I had not seen in a long time.

I remember a repairman was supposed to stop by that afternoon to take a look at the dishwasher, which had been leaking since

Monday. The lawn needed mowing. The neighbor's Callery pear trees had bloomed, saturating the block with the noxious smell of semen. There was a leak behind the fireplace that had developed sometime in February during a late-season snowstorm, and the area over the mantel had puckered, tea-colored stains spreading outward from the seam below the ceiling. White dust from the rotted drywall had seeped out, blooming over the bricks of the fireplace. That entire wall would have to be torn down and rebuilt.

I remember Tannhäuser throwing himself at Elisabeth's feet and refusing to tell her where he's been, no matter how much she begs. And I remember the way the joyful song of their reunion was lost to the roar of static.

Late in the afternoon, I tried to help my daughter with the unwritten essay.

Okay, I said, opening a new document on my laptop. Let's get this done so you can go see your aunts and your grandmother. They're all expecting you.

My girl slumped in the chair beside me.

This shouldn't be too hard to write, I said. You just have to write about what you think the call of the wild is.

I don't know what it is, my daughter said, pouting. I don't know what we're supposed to say.

There's nothing that you're *supposed* to say. There's no one right answer. It can be whatever you think it is.

Well, I don't know.

Come on, you can do this. Just think about it.

My daughter stared into space, silent. I rapped the table with my palm.

What?

Sit up.

Fine.

Could it be nature? Or instinct?

Maybe. I don't know.

You read the book, didn't you?

Yes.

Okay. Let's try the other essay question instead. In what way is the novel fervently American?

I can't answer that one either.

Why not?

Because I don't know what that means!

You just need to come up with a thesis, I said. You know how to do that, right?

No.

No?

They never taught us how.

That's impossible.

They always say to just write down the theme. And connect it to the main idea.

What does that even mean?

I don't know.

If you don't understand something they're teaching you, you need to ask more questions.

Okay.

Look, your thesis is essentially an argument. So what's your argument?

My daughter sighed loudly, dramatically. This is the most boring book I've ever read, she said. That's my argument.

That's not helpful.

She looked away and let her eyes settle on the chaos of the table and the unfinished game. Who had taught her to wait until the last minute like this? Certainly I hadn't.

Sweetheart, I began. How long have you known about this project?

No response.

Weeks? I pressed. Months?

She wouldn't speak. My Princess Turandot. She was freezing me out now, as if she couldn't hear me, or didn't care to. As if I weren't there at all.

Look, it's not so hard, I said. We decide what the call of the wild is, and then we say why we think that. So what do you think it could be?

I don't know. Nature or something. What was the other thing you said before?

Instinct.

Or instinct, I guess. Whatever you think it is.

Come on, you can do better than that. I know you're capable of doing brilliant things.

But Daddy, I don't *know*!

She was breathing hard now, whimpering between each exhaled gasp, her hands clenched into fists. I watched her for a while, waiting for her to collect herself, but she didn't.

Calm down. Just breathe.

I can't!

All right, all right, I said. Just relax. I'll help you write it.

She went slack then, her face as still and pale as a doll's.

Trust me, I told her. It's going to be great. *You're* going to be great.

My wife had left the room at some point — to do what, I didn't know. She seemed relaxed. I was surprised to see her so apparently unbothered by the looming deadline we were facing. Perhaps she was just trying to keep us calm. She'd always been the one who maintained order and smoothed the course, no matter what problems might befall us.

Beau, on the other hand, seemed jumpier than usual. He kept bristling at hints of sound. He stared at the squirrels that stood still on the lawn, growled low when they darted away.

We were still a real family that day, doing the exact kinds of things that real families do. The project would get done — the thesis would be generated, the essay would be written, the verdant paint on the mountains would dry, the clay wolves would find their homes among them — and we would all be relieved. My daughter would have her movie night in the haven of my mother's house, and my wife and I would have a Saturday evening to ourselves. It would all be fine.

All I had ever wanted was to do everything the right way. All I had wanted was the love and stability that had never been mine all through my miserable childhood. I had wanted to build a shell around my girls, so that they would never have to suffer as I had.

I had once truly believed that I could have a better life — I thought I had seen only the bright colors of happiness arrayed before me like a great garden of my own making. But I had been wrong. The good times had already come and gone, and the garden had given up its blooms before I knew to harvest them. I had destroyed our lives, just like my father had destroyed the lives of his own wife and children. This house I'd built with my own hands was decaying now, falling to pieces, and no amount of light or air could save it.

Unless.

Wasn't I still the hero of this story? Who was I if I couldn't shepherd us safely through a crisis? I had to make things right, for their sake. They were everything to me — they would always be everything.

I knew that we desperately needed an evening alone, my wife and I. As soon as we finished enough work on the project we could get our daughter out of there, pack her off to her grandmother and aunts. Then my wife and I would sit down together and I would finally tell her what had happened. I would open a bottle of wine and wait until she'd taken her first smiling, ruddy-tongued sips before saying anything.

Then I would lean toward her, brush the hair out of her face with the gentle blade of my hand, kiss the soft corner of her mouth, encase her in my arms so that she couldn't move, so that I could feel the sympathetic flutter of her sighs.

It's all a misunderstanding, I would say,

her head warm and silent against my chest. You know me, my love. You know I would never do those things. Could never.

With time I could make her see that our situation was just like that of poor Tannhäuser. He lost control of himself and sang to the assembled crowd a forbidden song of profane, ecstatic love. He was condemned to die, and certainly would have if not for Elisabeth. She pleads for mercy on his behalf, promising that the sinner she loves will achieve salvation through atonement. And she vows that if he fails, she will plead his case to God herself.

Her love for that poor sinner, that poor bastard — that was the kind of love my wife had for me. More powerful than any disaster. Insoluble. Indelible. I would beg for forgiveness, and my wife would forgive me. Because she loved me.

I held on to those thoughts, nursing them like a puncture wound in my chest as my girls and I continued our work, hymns of forgiveness assaulting us from the stereo.

The dishwasher repairman never came. It was after five now, and we were moving into the next stage of the evening. The dryer had completed its cycle and the duvet cover was a warm and pristine cloud of white once more. Beau snuffed and paced around the back door as he waited for his dinner. The little clay wolves had been glued into place among the snowcapped mountains of the board game, and we had composed a sufficiently robust outline unpacking the conflict between instinct and civilization in the novel, complete with key quotes for evidence. The essay would write itself in the morning.

The opera had ended, the pilgrims overwhelming us with their last breathtaking chorus, our speakers crackling with the final ferocious tremolo of the violins as I wiped my eyes with the back of my hand. I always cried when I listened to that final scene. My wife stretched out on the sofa and watched my daughter and me as we made our preparations to leave.

Don't forget your coat, darling.

It's so warm out, Mommy. I don't need one.

It will get cold later. You'll be cold.

No I won't.

My wife sighed, but she was smiling.

Come here then.

My daughter trotted over to the sofa, then bent and kissed my wife on her forehead with theatrical care and affection, as if she were the mother putting her little child to bed.

Au revoir, mon chéri.

À bientôt.

I didn't know it then, of course — none of us knew — but it was the last time my girls would ever see each other.

We were out of the house by six. The drive was uneventful, just the usual traverse down the sunbaked spine of the island — traffic slowing near the exit for the mall, then speeding up again as we approached the South Shore. The breeze became cooler, more forceful, and full of sea, gusts beating their way into the car through our half-open windows. My daughter crossed her thin goose-fleshed arms, but still wouldn't admit that she was cold, shaking her head when I asked.

I had made this journey south so many times, more times than I could possibly count. But though it was all so familiar, today I found myself noticing and appreciating each detail of the drive, especially as we drew closer to our destination: the old town with its diners and car dealerships, each landmark as decrepit and enduring as a Roman ruin; the winding lane flanked by high hedges, the shadowy passage under the canopy of trees that hid our crumbling

Victorian dollhouse from the street.

Perhaps I knew that these details would matter later, that it was important to remember them.

My sisters were waiting for us on the front porch. They were bare-legged in garish caftans, sipping from crystal goblets filled with crushed ice, cut fruit, and wine. They waved, leaning forward in their wicker rocking chairs as we exited the car.

Look who's here! Kit hooted.

My daughter raced up the wooden steps, but I hung back, leaning against the porch column.

We're so glad you could make it, Miss Call of the Wild.

Oh my *god,* my daughter moaned, collapsing into the empty rocker between my sisters. I thought we'd *never* finish it!

Is it all done?

No, I said. She's got more to do tomorrow.

That's why I can't sleep over, my daughter said, pouting. It's not fair.

Well, that's all right, Deedee said, waving everyone's disappointment away. You certainly don't have to think about it tonight.

What are we going to watch? What are we going to eat?

Whatever you want, baby girl.

Can we get sushi? Please?

Not Domino's?

Gross.

Oh, you used to love the cheesy bread, Kit teased. You used to dip it in the blue cheese sauce that came with the buffalo wings.

Not since, like, forever. That stuff is so bad for you.

One of these days you're going to get so skinny you'll disappear.

I listened to them banter. Their chatter was so light, so unencumbered by any kind of care. They would pass an evening eating salted edamame and spicy tuna rolls, watching the sort of movies that my daughter wasn't allowed to watch at home — movies about murderous cults of teenaged witches, or Shakespearean adaptations set in boarding schools. Maybe my sisters would read her cards, see what they could divine about her future. It would be a lovely evening, and when she finally came home that night, everything would be different.

How's Ma? I asked suddenly.

The girls turned to look at me, surprised to see me still standing there.

She's good, said Deedee. It's been a good day.

Do you want to see her? Kit asked. She's

293

up in her room, but I'm pretty sure she's awake.

I saw her then, there in the front hall. She's still in her pajamas, her messy hair leavened with morning light. Some crooner is crackling on the record player. Our father has his bearish arms locked around our mother's waist, and he is dipping her, burping nonsense into her neck as she throws her head back, away from him, casting her wild eyes around the room in search of aid, in search of us. And we are watching from the stairs, the twins shrieking with helpless, thoughtless laughter as Evie takes my hand and squeezes it until our knuckles crack.

I shook my head, shook the scene out of my eyes.

No, I said quickly. That's all right. Just give her my love.

But I still lingered, listening as the engine of their cheerful conversation turned over and restarted itself, continuing on down the road without me. I stood there waiting to say good-bye until I was sure I wouldn't choke on my words.

I'm heading out, I said finally, turning to go. Call me when you're ready to come home.

Okay, Daddy.

Not too late, sweetheart.

I know.

On my way back I made a few stops. First, the good wine store in our charming little downtown, where I took my time choosing two bottles from their extensive French selection — a thirty-three-dollar organic rosé from Provence, and a very fine sixty-four-dollar Bordeaux that we'd enjoyed a year or two ago on someone's birthday. My birthday or my wife's, I couldn't recall. Or maybe it had been Christmas. I wanted to remember, but I couldn't.

Next, I stopped in at the bakery down the street, where I bought their last baguette and a raspberry lemon tart. It was the kind of dessert that my wife liked, more sour than sweet. I got a full-size tart, so that there would be enough left over for my daughter when she came home later that night. At the last minute I asked for three croissants. For the morning.

Then, using my debit card, I swiped myself into the vestibule of my bank, where I took out four hundred dollars in twenties from the ATM. There was nothing unusual about this. I always kept cash in the house — some in my sock drawer, some under the mattress — and after my wanderings this week I needed to replenish my supply.

I made it to the florist just before it closed.

The dark elfin girl behind the counter helped me make a beautiful bouquet of hydrangeas — pearl white and palest blue, like something a bride would carry.

Just make sure you put them in lots of cold water, the girl called after me. Otherwise they'll be wilted by the morning.

I nodded, waved my thanks and good-bye without looking back. Outside it was evening — the warmth of the day had gone, and the streets of our town were gray and empty in the sudden gloaming.

There was no putting it off any longer. It was time for me to go home.

At this point I must pause to address some concerns, which are beginning to take on an increasingly uncomfortable and burdensome weight in my mind. Specifically, I am concerned that despite my best efforts to tell my story honestly, I may be missing the mark. Not telling it the way it should be told. Not coming off quite right. Owing to my present state of complete misery and remorse, I fear that I've made things look a certain way — cast things in a certain light, so to speak — and I know that way of looking is not entirely faithful to the reality of what actually happened, or how my girls and I actually lived our life together. As I've said before, I know it's impossible to fully capture the truth of it all, let alone communicate that truth to people who never even knew us. In the retelling, it's far too easy to miss the heart of it. But that doesn't stop me from wanting to get it right.

The truth is, my wife and I did make it to France. One summer, the year before our daughter was born. We spent a few days in Paris with her parents, days that I recall were a bit tense but pleasant as we got over our jet lag in their cramped and pungent apartment. Then the two of us took a train down to Aix-en-Provence, where my wife had gone to university. We rented an apartment with a terrace in a building that dated back to the Middle Ages, and we passed a romantic week wandering the narrow cobblestone lanes, hiking up to the scenic lookout point where Cézanne painted Mont Sainte-Victoire, drinking glasses of pallid, one-euro rosé in plazas while children kicked soccer balls and shouted to one another as dusk descended through the canopy of trees overhead.

I honestly don't remember much about the trip. I haven't even mentioned it until now because it hasn't seemed important, certainly not in the grand scheme of our life together. I do remember that my wife cried often while we were there. She cried when her mother served us couscous for dinner, a childhood favorite. She cried when I took a picture of her on the doorstep of the building where she'd lived as a student. She cried after we made love on our tiny terrace one night, her halting groans of pleasure giving way to sobs that were drowned out by the shouts of revelers below.

Whenever I asked her why she was crying, she would say that she was just so happy.

We meant to go back someday as a family, when our daughter was old enough to appreciate it. I know we would have eventually, maybe even as soon as the following summer. It would have been the perfect time — that elusive sweet spot at the beginning of adolescence, before our girl could finish growing up and leave us behind.

There was no reason we couldn't have.

When I got home I found my wife asleep in the living room where I'd left her, the dog nestled in the gap between her knees, his head resting on her thigh. They snored together, quietly and companionably. I stood in the doorway and watched them for a while, then lay down on the floor beside them, my spine pressed to the rug. I closed my own eyes and waited, letting the long minutes pass. I was reluctant to bring my wife back into wakefulness, because I knew what would happen when I did, and who knew when we would ever be at peace like this again?

Finally I roused myself. I knelt beside my wife, put out my hand, and stroked her hair and neck until she stirred and let out a soft little gasp before seeing me and smiling. She always made that sound when I woke her, no matter how gentle I tried to be. Looking at her now, I knew it wasn't time yet.

Let me cook for us tonight, I murmured. You're too tired.

Eyes closed once more, she nodded in assent. In another moment she was dozing again.

There was a flank steak in the freezer. I set it in the sink under lukewarm running water to defrost, and then I gathered ingredients to make a salad. That and the baguette I'd bought would have to serve us. I opened the wine to let it breathe. The bottle I'd picked out really deserved a special meal, but we would have to live with what I could make. I kept the radio off — for once I didn't feel like listening to anything. I cleared everything out of the dining room, moving the still-drying board game to the coffee table in the living room. Then I began to make dinner.

I find it difficult to describe this part of it. These hours. The meal I made for us, the dinner we had together that night. I find this period much harder to describe than many of the other things that happened. I can't tell you why.

I can tell you how to cook a steak, though — how I cooked our steak that night. Once the meat is defrosted and brought up to room temperature you blot it with paper towels, pressing the flesh until it's dry. Then you season aggressively with salt and pepper — if you think you're using too much, that's probably just the right amount. Heat a pan on high for a few minutes, until it starts to smoke — cast iron is best if you have it, which you should. Throw the steak in the pan and cook for two minutes on each side, not a second more. Set it on a cutting board and let it rest for another minute or so while you finish setting the table. Then carve. If you follow these steps it will be an impeccable medium rare.

That was the way my wife liked it.

I cut into the meat with our best carving knife, that first slice of the blade parting the charred exterior to reveal the rich ruby within. Perfect, as usual. When I finished getting everything ready I called to my wife,

300

and we sat down at the dining room table together.

Things began to go wrong almost immediately. My torso suddenly tingled and burned with an uncontrollable itch, as if I had rolled around in poison sumac, or a colony of biting ants. I scratched at myself, pinching and clawing at my breast, then stood, nearly knocking over my chair.

Excuse me, I said, backing away from the table. I'm sorry, love.

Darling? my wife called after me. What's wrong?

Nothing! I responded, my voice light. Nothing's wrong.

But darling —

I just need a moment!

I locked myself in the downstairs bathroom and stripped off my shirt, fully expecting to look into the mirror and see a raw and vicious rash overtaking and disfiguring me — but there was nothing at all.

It was just me. Just my body.

I splashed cold water on my chest and neck, slapped my bare skin hard enough to leave a flush of handprints. Naked from the waist up, I stared at myself in the mirror for a long time, waiting until my lungs stopped pulsing grotesquely between the barriers of my ribs, waiting until I could control my face again.

Then I put my shirt back on and returned to my wife.

Is everything all right?

Yes, I said evenly. Everything is fine.

I sat down at the table again and began to cut my meat into pieces, but I found I couldn't bring myself to eat them. My tongue felt heavy and distended in my mouth; the wine tasted unbearably sour, but I continued drinking it. The itching had subsided, but a nauseating shiver kept passing through my body, a subtle convulsion that felt almost sexual. My wife was talking, but I couldn't hear or understand a word that she was saying. I was in that deaf and distant place again, watching my life from behind thick glass. Impotent.

Just begin somehow, I told myself. *Just say something. Just say her name.*

Darling?

I looked up. She was watching me closely, her doelike eyes dark with concern.

What's wrong?

Nothing, I said. I told you there's nothing.

Why aren't you eating?

I looked down at my plate. The shredded, exsanguinated flesh looked like something you would feed to a dog. I choked back a long swallow of wine. I opened my mouth, then closed it again. I was afraid I might begin to sob, or scream. With a sigh I leaned forward and took my wife's hands, kneaded her wrists with my thumbs, tried to find the words for what I had to tell her.

What's wrong, darling? she murmured. You can tell me.

I shook my head. I couldn't.

I'm sorry, love, I said. I'm sorry.

I closed my eyes and took a breath.

I'm just so tired.

We were silent for a while. My shivering intensified — I knew I had to get my body under control, force it through its motions. Command it.

Let's go upstairs, I said suddenly. Let's go to bed.

Right now?

Yes, I said, still holding her hands, pulling them to me. I've wanted you all day.

We should clean up first.

No we shouldn't, I said.

But — you're shaking.

I know. I want you right now.

There was something uncertain in her face now. A sense of stiffness, of hesitation. It disturbed me. Why now, when she had never questioned me like this before? If only she would trust me, I could fix this mess. I knew that everything would be all right once we were in bed together, once she was safe in my arms. I could convince her of everything then.

Come on, I said, looking into her eyes. Come.

For a long time we simply stared at one another. In those moments I feared that we were already lost to each other, but I also knew that if I could just stay strong and outlast her she would relent.

Come, I repeated.

Then she softened to me. I saw the moment of her decision — her submission — saw it in her wet and shining eyes, the way she let her body relax back into its natural state of gentleness. The way I always knew her to be. She leaned toward me, her forehead nearly touching mine, close enough that I could feel the breath of her words against my lips.

Let me take a shower, she said, her voice low. Then I'll meet you in the bedroom.

She went up, leaving the table untouched. In the kitchen, I listened to the shower run above me — I thought of drinking the rosé, but instead I filled a rocks glass with Laphroaig. It tasted like nothing. I drank one, then another, then more. Within a few minutes I had finished the bottle, which I left in the sink.

Finally I climbed the stairs to our room. I lay down on our bed, which seemed to pitch and roll beneath me. I held on to the edges of the mattress and closed my eyes against the unsteady tide that seemed to bear me ever closer to shipwreck and disaster. As I lay there, my thoughts turned, once more, to the final act of *Tannhäuser*. I thought of poor saintly Elisabeth, who has been waiting so long for her love to return to her. I thought of her hope when she sees the pilgrims approaching, her mounting dread as she searches each hooded face, her despair as she realizes her beloved sinner has failed in his quest for absolution and has not come back to her. She knows then that she will have to die to save him.

And then I knew with a terrible certainty that my wife would leave me.

How had I not realized it before now? All the evidence had been there, right in front of me. The messages I'd seen on her phone, her casual quickness in closing her browser windows these past few weeks — only now did I understand the significance of those minor clues. Even her sweet compliance was nothing more than a ploy. She had been making plans for a long time, and now everything had driven me to the point where

I had to confess, and the awful shame of what I had done to us would be the final push she needed to leave me forever.

I suddenly saw the pale hart's antler of her left hand, the way it had looked in her lap that night in front of the fire — defiantly naked, unadorned by any evidence of my love, of our commitment. I saw it all now: her eyes downcast in disappointment, not modesty. Her long silences, weighted with regret. The way she carried herself in a crowd of strangers — showing off, seeking. The way her body would recoil at my mere approach. She hadn't worn my ring in months, and it was because she had already made up her mind.

She knew exactly who she had married — who I really was.

Desperate, I reasoned there had to be a way to make her stay. There had to be a way that I could convince her not to leave me.

Forgive me. Forgive me. I've made a terrible mistake. I don't deserve you. I don't even deserve to live. I'm sorry. Just forgive me. Stay. Please.

The door opened. There she was, her dark hair wet, her silk robe open to show her damp skin. She came toward me with sly eyes, smiling in her soft way.

O thou, my fair evening star.

No — a cat caught eating the canary.

I stood. Before she could speak, I put my hands on her throat.

And I swear on everything that I once held dear in my wretched life that she seemed to relax into my grip, that she surrendered herself to me. As if she'd known, somehow, all along.

The summer Evie was fourteen she was infatuated with the androgynously handsome lead singer of a mediocre British goth-rock band. She bought all of the band's albums on both vinyl and cassette and scrawled their brooding lyrics over every surface she could touch — her notebooks, her bedroom walls, the toes and soles of her sneakers. Even her underwear was marked by this man's words, obscure slant-rhymed couplets about drugs and failed relationships penned onto the cotton. I had never seen a lust like that before, had never known that someone could be so hungry with such impossible desire, least of all my older sister.

She had never been like that in our own games.

In August the singer's face and naked torso appeared on the cover of a major popular music magazine. The object of my sister's obsession lay in rumpled white sheets, his sharp cheekbones kissed by late-morning light, his dark hair tousled perhaps in agitation, perhaps by the hands of an unseen lover. His rakish eyes flashed, pleading with you to come back to bed, to stay a bit longer. He bit his lip, waiting. To Evie, it was a picture of pure sex.

The issue sold out immediately. After two weeks of searching every newsstand and bookstore within a bikeable radius of our house, Evie walked into our public library wearing one of our father's shirts, an old chambray oxford that was much too big for her. A few minutes later, she walked out with the library's copy of the magazine tucked into the front of her denim shorts, her beloved's face pressed against her stomach and hips, finally hers.

But Evie hated the rest of the cover. She was repulsed by the red and black text that advertised other bands she hated and stories she would not read. All the headlines and teasers were pollutants, and they soiled the perfection of her love.

So she tried to free him from his bonds.

We sat on her bed and I watched as she took a pair of our mother's nail scissors and began to snip carefully at the cover, pruning the words away, leaving the celestial face and body intact.

Trust me, she whispered to the lover cradled in her lap. This will be so much better.

Maybe I shifted then, trying to get more comfortable, or to get a better look. Or maybe Evie was the one who moved, crossing her legs beneath her or propping herself on an elbow.

Whatever the reason, in the next moment my sister's hand slipped, and before she could stop herself she had sliced a thick scar through her beloved's rosy left nipple.

For a long moment Evie was completely still and silent. I watched her pale face fearfully, waiting for her reaction. She let herself fall backward onto her pillows, lay as though she were dead — the same way she had been when I saw her with our father. It was as if she were not herself, not Evie anymore, just someone else's body that didn't move.

But then she raised herself up with a sharp gasp and began to howl.

It was a hoarse moan that tightened into a shriek and went on and on, a sound worse than anything I'd ever heard. Her face was grim and horrible, lit with an indescribable passion, and she gripped the scissors until her fingertips lost their blood and she slashed and shredded the image of the one she loved, the one she could not have and would never have, until all that remained were a few handfuls of ragged scraps spilled over the bed. All this time I watched her — even when she screamed at me to stop looking at her, screamed at me to go and leave her alone, I didn't move.

I stayed — not consoling her, not even trying to calm her — just watching her. And when my sister had finally spent her rage we listened to her breathing rend the silence around us, each labored inhale like something too heavy that she'd been forced to drag too far for too long.

She was still breathing. I could still hear it.

When I tried to stand up she grabbed at me, her hand clutching at my ankle in a violent spasm, but I kicked myself free. I pulled the sheets and comforter off the bed, threw them down into a pile on the floor, covering everything but her bare feet.

I still could have stopped, then. But really, I couldn't have.

The billy club was under my side of the bed. It had been there for weeks, growing a delicate skin of dust. I reached for it now, wiped it with the hem of my T-shirt. The collar had been stretched out beyond saving, and blood from my nose had stained the cotton. I would have to change and throw the garment away.

With the club I hit what was under the pile of bedding until it stopped moving, until the sound of the blows became muffled and wet. Then I lay down on the bed and blacked out.

and was. Then I lay down on the bed and blacked out.

When I woke up again she had come back. She stood at the foot of the bed, still wearing her robe. We looked at each other in the gray light of the early morning that hung like smoke in the room.

I thought you left, I said.

She shrugged, made a vague gesture.

You came back.

She didn't answer me right away. She kept looking at me, kept herself very still, her eyes a flat and unblinking black. She held her breath.

I had to, she said finally. I left all my things.

Your things?

She pointed to the rumpled pile of bedding on the floor.

But that's not — I said. That's — no. That isn't yours. Those aren't your things.

She shook her head then, slowly touched

314

her fingertips to her throat.
Then what is it?

A phone was going off somewhere. A hard buzzing against wood, loud digital chimes ascending and descending. My arms and legs jerked and I was awake again. My eyes ranged over the blank ceiling, the black windows with their curtains drawn back, exposing me to the night. For a moment I didn't know where I was — it was possible I had been unconscious for days.

It was cold. There was a bad smell in the room that I couldn't name.

The phone was still going off, the sound lodged somewhere deep inside my head. No. It was somewhere close to me. I threw my hand back behind my head, fumbled blindly over the cluttered surface of the bedside table. There. Holding it to my face, I realized that it wasn't my phone — it was someone else's — but I answered it anyway, my numb fingers probing the screen in a pattern I didn't know I remembered.

Yes, I said. It's me.

I was convinced that I was still asleep. That I was way, way down in the deepest part of a dream. That I hadn't even begun to make my way back to the surface.

Daddy?

Her voice brought me back. I caught my breath.

Yes, sweetheart.

Why are you on Mommy's phone?

My girl, I thought. *My girl.*

She's asleep, love, I said. What's up?

Oh. Well, can you pick me up now?

Now everything else was starting to come back. It was all beginning to surface, dead fish floating up from deep water. I avoided looking at the floor, even though I knew what was there.

Of course, dear, I said carefully. I'm leaving now. I'll be there very soon.

The phone went silent against my ear. I regarded the device for a few minutes, turning it over in my hand, trying to decide what to do with it. Finally I powered it down and put it in my pocket. Perhaps I would throw it away later, somewhere else.

I changed out of my ruined T-shirt. This too I hesitated over before leaving it balled up on the bathroom floor — I would deal with it later. I put on an old blue-and-gray flannel, a garment I almost never wore unless I was sick or doing work around the house. I turned out the light in the bedroom and shut the door behind me.

Downstairs I spent a while searching for my daughter's winter coat, the pink puffer one. She would need it now that it had gotten so cold out; before I had powered the phone down I had seen the weather icon on the screen indicating that the temperature had dropped down into the forties. It seemed unthinkable that only a few hours ago it had felt like high summer.

I left everything the way it was — the abandoned meal on the dining room table, the school project in the living room — only turning off the lights as I made my way through each room. It would all be dealt with later, somehow. I finally found the pink puffer coat hanging on a hook near the side door, under a dark olive trench coat and some other jackets and sweaters that had been worn by other people more recently. The dog's leash was there as well — I took it in hand, then put on my own coat.

I believe it was at this point that I realized I was carrying the billy club around with me. It hung loosely at my side, an extension of my right arm. I didn't examine it as closely as I had the phone or my shirt. I simply set it down on the kitchen counter for a moment, then called to my dog.

He was upstairs, pawing at the bedroom door, yipping loudly and fretfully. When he heard me calling he hurried to the landing to peer down beseechingly at me. I crawled up the stairs on my hands and knees, stayed crouched down low and beckoned to my dog, cooing endearments.

Come here, I murmured, reaching out for him. Good boy, good boy. Come here.

Finally he approached me with a halting gait, came close enough to let me fondle his bowed head. He was a small dog, had probably been the runt of the litter. Years ago, when we'd first brought him home from the shelter, he'd crawled under the sofa and slept there for an hour before finally allowing us to coax him out, to hold and love him.

Come on, boy, I said. Let's go out.

I notched my fingers under his collar and clipped the retractable leash on, then led him downstairs — his curly head hesitating over the precipice of each step, his paws making their soft, syncopated thuds as we descended. We went into the kitchen.

I was careless — I had given the leash too much slack and held it too loosely, and when my dog saw the club in my hand he jerked away and out of my grip, the leash retracting with a snap, its plastic handle clattering after him as he scuttled away. I chased him for several awkward, lunging laps around the kitchen island — clockwise, then counterclockwise, then clockwise again — each swing of the club a moment too late, a beat too slow. Finally I feinted right, then darted left, snatching the handle of the leash just before it got away from me again.

Breathing harder now, I stood and wound the thin cord of the leash around and around my wrist, pulling my dog to me across the hardwood floor, just close enough so that I could land the blow.

I don't remember leaving my house, or any details of the drive south. At some point I glanced behind me and saw that I had placed the billy club on the backseat, partly covering it with my daughter's pink coat. The bright beams of the streetlights kept slicing through the car, jumping over the mound of the coat and club. I faced forward again and kept my eyes on the road.

I thought idly of where my daughter and I would go and how we would rebuild our life together once I had her with me again. I decided not to worry about specifics just then. Together, we would make our plans and find a way to get over our pain.

I thought of a television spot I'd seen once for Homesteader, a real estate search engine. Our agency hadn't made the ad, but I'd greatly admired it. The commercial was the kind of work I aspired to, a poignant and compelling story that stayed with the viewer long after its images had receded from the screen. No small achievement these days.

The ad's opening scene takes place in a darkened kitchen, where a man sits at the counter, looking at his laptop. The light of the screen illuminates his somber face as he searches houses for sale, clicking through slideshows of cottages with picket fences, bungalows with big trees in their front yards. He frowns.

The man's young daughter comes in wearing pajamas, a bedraggled teddy bear dangling from her small hand. He turns and speaks to her.

We'll try to find something near Grandma, okay?

His daughter seems not to hear him, disregarding him, as if she doesn't care to listen. She turns away to look at something else, then takes her father's hand and pulls him to the window, points up at the night sky.

I think that star is Mommy, she says. It's the brightest.

We cut to a new scene now, later on that same night. The man is back on his computer, using Homesteader to create highly individualized preferences and parameters. His features soften. He smiles at something unseen.

New scene. In the warm vestibule of a new house, the girl runs into her grandmother's waiting arms. They are happy.

That night on the front porch, the father gazes up at the stars, his daughter standing on the lawn before him, her hands raised to the sky. The camera zooms in on the brightest star above.

Good night, Mommy, the girl whispers.

When I arrived I hesitated out front for a while. I stood shivering in the driveway, listening to the walls of dark pines breathing around me, watching for signs of life in the old house. I took in the dark gabled windows, the missing shutters, the rotten columns of the porch where I once lay sobbing and powerless as my father had his way with my sister. From where I stood I could look in and just make out the television in the living room, its weak and stuttering light flitting against the walls like a trapped bird.

I looked up above me, but I could see no stars — the sky had clouded over, paling to a warm, unearthly mauve. Soon it would begin to snow.

In that moment, I decided that I should leave my daughter behind. I knew that she would be safe here, surrounded by the strange and broken women who loved her. They may have had their flaws, but they would do their best to take care of her. They would chip away at her inchoate anorexia, fattening her up with their relentless cooking and feeding. They would launder her uniforms every Sunday and see that she stayed at Hutch, where her clan of girlfriends would close ranks around her, precious survivor of unspeakable tragedy. Teachers would go easy on her; therapists would help her get through the worst of it. And perhaps one day she would write about what had happened to us, just as beautiful, brave Evie had intended to write her own sad story, before she gave up and jumped.

The truth was that I didn't deserve to see my daughter grow up and become a woman. Not after what I had done to us.

But who would take care of them if I were gone?

No, I thought. No. Whatever might happen to us now, my daughter belonged with me. There was no truth deeper than that.

I let myself in through the unlocked door, my daughter's coat slung over my shoulder, its soft sleeves dangling against my chest. In the front hall I turned away from the murk of my reflection in the credenza mirror, and with careful quiet steps I passed through the French doors and into the lightless living room where my sisters lay lumped together on the sofa like dogs, snoring in guttural wheezes. On the television screen two teenagers in parochial school uniforms — a black boy and a blond girl — were arguing fiercely, their attractive, tearstained faces drawn close, as if to kiss. My mother was nowhere to be seen.

If anyone else had been awake — if I'd had to speak with my sisters, or see my mother — I still may have given it all up, even then. But the only soul stirring was my girl, huddled in the rose-patterned wingback chair that dwarfed her little body, her dark eyes glazed with sleep as she gazed at the escalating fight on the television screen. I stood and watched her for a while. Even then — even then — I still could have stopped.

I whispered her name.

She looked up. Saw me. I beckoned to her with a nod, and she got up out of the chair and approached me, yawning widely. I put my arm around her, draped her coat around her shoulders — together we walked out of the house, and my daughter let out a little gasp.

It's *snowing*?

It was. We stood and watched the flakes drift through the streetlight, specks of static falling and falling through the night. It fell on our shoulders and hair, too soft and light to chill us. The silence was smothering and complete, thick against our ears. My daughter did a little twirl, as if she were playing the role of an enchanted girl, and I thought I saw Evie again, performing for us — for me — as she always had.

In the car I made sure my daughter buckled up. The billy club was still resting on the backseat, hidden in a lean-to of shadow. As I drove away I looked back at the house once, briefly. I was reasonably sure that I would never see it again.

My daughter fell asleep beside me almost immediately, and as I accelerated westward down the abandoned road I let my thoughts race on unencumbered. It was just after midnight — I could drive all through the night, and by early morning we would be far away. The Canadian border was only seven or so hours north, and there would be no traffic. Perhaps we could go to Montreal — I had never been there myself, but I'd heard good things. I hadn't packed anything for us, but it didn't matter. I had my wallet, so we would be able to buy whatever we needed for our new start. I imagined a tree-lined street in a new city, a bilingual girls' school, two pairs of scuffed snow boots waiting by our back door.

The worst was over now. It would be hard to move forward, but in the end we would be all right.

But I hadn't taken our passports. They'd been right there, stashed in the drawer of my bedside table, but I hadn't thought to take them with me when I left the house. I hadn't been thinking at all.

I looked over at my daughter, and then I knew that there were other problems, insurmountable ones that I hadn't let myself face until now.

What would I say when she asked for her mother? What could I possibly tell her? I knew in my heart that there was nothing I could say, that no possible explanation would make it all right. And now it was much too late to bring her back.

I had changed my mind about that, anyway. I no longer saw that house as a safe haven for my girl. She would wither away there. Her life would be nothing like what I had wanted for her. My family didn't have the means or wherewithal to take care of her. They couldn't even take care of themselves. Soon my ailing mother would die, and my sisters would fully capitulate to their trash mysticism and squalid sloth. Money would run out, and my daughter would have to go to the unfathomably lousy district school, if my sisters even bothered sending her to school at all. She would end up just like the twins, stunted and perverted, shut into that crumbling sanatorium for the rest of her life, which would really be no kind of life at all.

Or she would end up like Evie, reckless with a rage that she would never fully understand, stumbling headlong toward drugs and johns and her own self-immolation, forever mauled by her trauma.

That couldn't happen to my daughter. I couldn't bear to imagine her alone in a world so full of peril, without me there to protect her. She couldn't live like that, failed by everyone who loved her.

She couldn't live knowing that I was the one who had killed her mother.

I didn't think anymore. I was calm. Blank. I made the turn onto the parkway, drove us over the bridge. I knew there was water down there, churning below us, but it was too dark to see it.

At the beach I parked close to the rail, just behind the wall of the dunes. I put out my hand and stroked my daughter's shoulder, watched her stir. She let out a little moan as she peered into the impenetrable darkness outside her window. Then she turned to me, her eyes still squinted shut, still half asleep.

Where are we?

Come on, I whispered. Let's walk for a little while.

She was too tired to resist, to ask any more questions. She was my daughter, and she trusted me.

It would all be over soon.

We got out of the car, walked a little way out onto beach. I reached for my daughter's hand and we looked out over the white-capped waves, the snow dancing around us. She yawned, leaned her head against my chest. I held her close as she shivered.

Daddy?

What, love?

I'm tired.

Then lie down, I said.

Right here?

Sure, I said. Here, I'll lie down with you.

We lay down together, shoulder-to-shoulder. The sand still held a hint of warmth from the heat of the day, even as the snow fell soft on our faces. We gazed up, watched the blinding swirls come down on us from the dark, melting before they reached the ground.

Can we go home?

Soon, sweetheart, I promised. Soon. Isn't this beautiful?

She didn't answer — she had fallen asleep again. Very gently, I turned her onto her side and covered her as much as I could with my coat.

I walked to the car and retrieved the club from the backseat. Then I hurried back. The last image I have is of a dark mound on the sand. The back of a dark head.

Everyone uses the photograph of us on the beach.

It's sunset, and the flash has turned us into ghosts against a red sky.

My wife is farthest away, wrenching herself toward the water, her slender arm raised in what looks like a wave of farewell.

My daughter is between us, her hands gripping ours, holding us together.

And I'm closest to you, my chin raised in confidence and my eyes bright with pride, trying hard to look like a good man.

That was me. That was my family.

Club in hand, I walked quickly across the windswept beach, but not so quickly that I could hear my breath, or the beating of my heart.

It was a mercy that I only had to hit her once.

ACKNOWLEDGMENTS

Thank you to:

Julia Kenny, my dauntless, dedicated, visionary agent, for loving this book and working so hard to get it into the world; Veronique Baxter in the UK; and everyone else at Dunow, Carlson, and Lerner.

Margaux Weisman, my incredible editor, for understanding exactly what I wanted to say and helping me say it even better; Patrick Nolan, for having total faith in this project; and the brilliant design, editorial, and marketing teams at Penguin.

Jason Arthur and everyone at William Heinemann, for championing this novel early on.

Paul D'Amato and Myra Greene, for encouraging me to write when I wasn't really supposed to.

Ren Khodzhayev, for the essential reading recommendation.

Aloisia, whose farm was the perfect writer's residence.

Lilly Atlihan and the entire Beyrer clan, for always welcoming me into their home.

My family: Jonah, Emma, CJ, and my parents, Susan and Eric.

Sara J. Winston, for the original spark and the years of sincere enthusiasm thereafter.

And Edwin Aponte, my first and best reader, who believed in this story, and my ability to tell it, before I had written a word.

ABOUT THE AUTHOR

Ani Katz is a writer, photographer, and teacher. She was born and raised on the South Shore of Long Island, New York, and holds an MFA in photography from Columbia College Chicago and a BA from Yale. She lives in Brooklyn.